For more than forty years,
Yearling has been the leading name
in classic and award-winning literature
for young readers.

Yearling books feature children's
favorite authors and characters,
providing dynamic stories of adventure,
humor, history, mystery, and fantasy.

Trust Yearling paperbacks to entertain,
inspire, and promote the love of reading
in all children.

## OTHER YEARLING BOOKS YOU WILL ENJOY

BALLET SHOES, *Noel Streatfeild*

DANCING SHOES, *Noel Streatfeild*

THEATER SHOES, *Noel Streatfeild*

ALL-OF-A-KIND FAMILY, *Sydney Taylor*

THE SECRET GARDEN, *Frances Hodgson Burnett*

# Skating Shoes

## Noel Streatfeild

A YEARLING BOOK

Visit us on the Web! www.randomhouse.com/kids

Educators and librarians, for a variety of teaching tools, visit us at www.randomhouse.com/teachers

Library of Congress Cataloging-in-Publication Data
Streatfeild, Noel.
Skating shoes / Noel Streatfeild.
p. cm.
Summary: Nine-year-old Harriet Johnson goes ice-skating to strengthen her legs after an illness, befriends Lalla, the orphaned daughter of a great figure skating star, and finds encouragement to become a champion.
ISBN 978-0-394-80881-9 (trade) — ISBN 978-0-394-90881-6 (lib. bdg.) — ISBN 978-0-440-47731-0 (mass-market pbk.)
[1. Ice skating—Fiction. 2. Friendship—Fiction. 3. Orphans—Fiction. 4. Self-actualization (Psychology)—Fiction.] I. Title.
PZ7.S914Sk 2009
[Fic]—dc22 2009021803

Printed in the United States of America

10 9 8 7 6 5 4

First Yearling Edition

## Contents

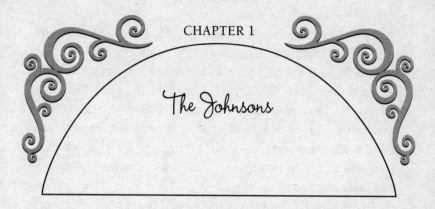

CHAPTER 1

The Johnsons

EVEN WHEN THE last of the medicine bottles were cleared away and she was supposed to have "had" convalescence, Harriet did not get well. She was a thin child with big brown eyes and a lot of reddish hair that did not exactly curl, but had a wiriness that made it stand back from her face rather like Alice's hair in *Alice in Wonderland*. Since her illness Harriet had looked all eyes, hair, and legs, and seemed to have no face at all—so much so that her brothers Alec, Toby and Edward said she had turned into a daddy-longlegs. Mrs. Johnson, whose name was Olivia, tried to scold the boys for teasing Harriet, but her scolding was not very convincing, because inside she could not help feeling that if a daddy-longlegs had a lot of hair and big eyes it would look very like Harriet.

Harriet's father was named George Johnson. He had a shop. It was not a usual sort of shop, because what it sold was entirely dependent on what his brother William grew, shot or caught. There had been a time when the Johnson family was rich. They had owned a large house in the country with plenty of land round it, and some fishing and shooting. The children's great-grandfather had not been able to afford to live in the big house, so he had built himself a smaller house on the edge of his property and rented the big house to other people. When his eldest son, the children's grandfather, came into the property he could not afford to live even in the new smaller house, so he brought up the children's father and their Uncle William in the lodge by the gates. But when he was killed in a motor accident and the children's Uncle William inherited the property, he was so poor he could not afford to live even in the lodge. So Uncle William decided the cheapest plan would be to live in two rooms in the house that his grandfather had built, and to rent the lodge.

When he had thought of this he said to his brother George, the children's father, "I tell you what, young feller me lad,"—he was the sort of man who spoke that way—"I'll keep a nice chunk of garden and a bit of shootin' and fishin' and I'll make the garden pay, and you can have the produce, trout from the river, and game from the woods, and keep a shop in London and sell it, and before you can say 'Bob's me uncle' you'll be a millionaire."

It did not matter how often anyone said "Bob's your uncle" for George did not become a millionaire. Uncle William had not married, and lived very comfortably in his two rooms in the smaller house on the edge of his estate, but one reason why he lived so comfortably was that he ate the best of everything that he grew, caught or shot. The result of this was that George and Olivia and the children lived very leanly indeed on the proceeds of the shop. It was not only that William ate everything worth eating that made life so hard for them, but also that people who buy in shops expect to go to special places for special things. When they are buying fruit they do not expect to be asked if they could do with a nice rabbit or a trout, especially when the rabbit and the trout are not very nice because the best ones have been eaten by an Uncle William.

The children's father was an optimist by nature, and he tried to believe that he could not be a failure and that anything he started would succeed in the end. He also had a deep respect and trust for his brother William.

"Don't let's get downhearted, Olivia," he would say. "It's all a matter of time and educating the public. The public can be educated to anything if only they're given time."

Olivia very seldom argued with George. She was not an arguing sort of person, and anyway she was very fond of him, but she did sometimes wonder if they would not all starve before the public could be taught to buy old, tired grouse which had been too tough for Uncle William, when what they had come to buy was vegetables.

One of the things that was most difficult for Olivia, and indeed for the whole family, was that what would not sell had to be eaten. This made a great deal of trouble because Uncle William had a large appetite and seldom sent more than one of any kind of fish or game, and the result was that the family meals were made up of several different kinds of food, which meant a lot of cooking.

"What is there for lunch today, Olivia?" George would ask, usually adding politely, "Sure to be delicious."

Olivia would answer, "There's enough rabbit for two, there is a very small pike, there is grouse—but I don't really know about that, it seems to be very, very old, as if it had been dead a long time—and there's sauerkraut. I'm afraid everybody must eat cabbage of some sort today. We've had over seven hundred from Uncle William this week, and it's only Wednesday."

One of the worst things to Harriet about having been ill was that she was not allowed to go to school, and her mother would not let her help in the house.

"Do go out, darling, you look so terribly thin and spindly.

Why don't you go down to the river? I know it's rather dull by yourself, but you like watching boats go by."

Harriet did like watching boats go by and was glad that her father had chosen to have his shop in outer London near the Thames, so she could see boats go by. But boat-watching is a summer thing, and Harriet was unlucky in that she had been ill all summer and was putting up with the getting-well stage in the autumn. Nobody, she thought, could want to go and look at a river in the autumn.

One particularly beastly day, when it looked every minute as if it were going to rain and never quite did, Harriet was coming home from the river feeling as blue as a lobelia, when a car stopped beside her.

"Hullo, Harriet. How are you getting on?"

Harriet had been so deep in gloom because she was cold and tired that she had not noticed the car, but as he spoke she saw Doctor Phillipson. Quite suddenly everything she had been thinking about spindly legs and fresh air and not going to school came over her in a wave and she did what she would never have done in the ordinary way: she told the doctor exactly what she thought of his treatment.

"How would you feel if you were made to walk up and down a river in almost winter, all by yourself, getting colder and colder, and bored-er and bored-er, with absolutely nothing to do, and not allowed to stay indoors for one minute because you'd been ill and your doctor said you'd got to have fresh air? I feel simply terrible, and I shouldn't think I'll ever, ever get well again."

The doctor was a nice, friendly sort of man, and clever-looking. Usually he was too busy to do much talking, but this time he seemed in a talking mood. He opened the door of his car and told Harriet to hop into the seat beside him; he had a visit or two to make and then he would take her home.

"I must say," he agreed, "you do look a miserable little specimen. I hoped you'd pick up after that convalescent home the hospital sent you to."

Harriet looked at him sadly, for she thought he was too nice to be so ignorant.

"I don't see why I should have got better at that convalescent home."

"It's a famous place."

"But it's at the top of a cliff, and everything goes on at the bottom of the cliff, sea-bathing and the sands and everything nice like that. I could never go down because my legs were too wobbly to bring me back."

The doctor muttered something under his breath which sounded like "idiots," and then he said:

"Haven't you any relations in the country that you could go and stay with for a bit?"

"No, we've only Uncle William. He's got only two rooms and use of a bathroom, and one of his two rooms is his kitchen. He shoots and catches and grows the things Daddy sells in the shop. Mummy says it's a pity he wouldn't have room for me because he eats all the best things and all that food would do me good, but I don't think it would because I'm not very hungry."

The doctor thought about Harriet's father's shop and sighed. He could well believe Uncle William ate the best of everything, for the shop looked as though he did. The Johnsons lived over the shop. There was not a great deal of room for a family of six. There was a kitchen dining-room, there was a living room, one bedroom for the three boys, a slip of a room for Harriet and a bedroom for George and Olivia. All he said was:

"You tell your father and mother I'll be along to have a talk with them this evening."

Since she had been ill Harriet had been made to go to bed at the same time as Edward, which was half-past six. This was a terrible insult, because Edward was only just seven, whereas she was nine and a half. So when Doctor Phillipson arrived, only Alec and Toby were up. Olivia was in the kitchen cooking the things George had not sold, Alec and Toby were doing their homework at one side of the table in the living room, and on the other side their father tried to work out the accounts. The days when their father did the accounts were bad days for Alec's and Toby's homework, since accounts were not their father's strong point.

"Alec, if I charge ninepence each for four hundred cabbages, and twopence a pound for four dozen bundles of carrots, three and sixpence each for eight rabbits, and thirty shillings for miscellaneous fish, and we've only sold a quarter of the carrots, half the cabbages, one of the rabbits, and all the fish but three, but we've made a very nice profit on mushrooms, how much have I earned?"

Toby, who was eleven and had what his schoolmaster called a mathematical brain, was driven into a frenzy by these problems of his father's. Toby was short-sighted and had to wear spectacles, and a piece of his sandy-colored hair was inclined to stand upright on the crown of his head. When his father asked questions about the finances of the shop, Toby's eyes would glare from behind his spectacles, and the piece of hair on the crown of his head would stand bolt upright like a guardsman on parade. He would be in such a hurry to explain to his father that a mathematical problem could not be presented in that form that his first words fell out on top of each other.

"But-Father-you-haven't-told-Alec-the-price of the mushrooms on which the whole problem hangs, nor the individual prices of the fish!"

It was in the middle of one of these arguments that Olivia brought Doctor Phillipson in. In spite of having to cook all the things Uncle William sent which would not sell, Olivia succeeded in looking at all times as if she were a hostess entertaining a very nice and amusing house party. In the kitchen she always wore a smock but underneath she had pretty clothes; they were usually very old because there was seldom money for new clothes, but she had a way of putting them on and of wearing them which seemed to say "Yes, isn't this pretty? How lucky I am to have nice clothes and time to wear them." As she ushered Doctor Phillipson into the living room it ceased to be full of George, Alec and Toby all arguing at the the tops of their voices, and of Alec's and Toby's school books, and George's dirty little bits of paper on which he kept his accounts. Suddenly she was showing a guest into a big, gracious drawing-room.

"Doctor Phillipson's come to talk to us about Harriet."

The Johnson children were properly brought up. Alec and Toby jumped to their feet murmuring "Good evening, sir," and Alec gave the doctor a chair facing George.

The doctor came straight to the point.

"Harriet is not getting on. Have you any relations in the country you could send her to?"

George, though he only had two, offered the doctor a cigarette.

"But of course, my dear fellow, my brother William has a splendid place; love to have her."

The doctor was sure George would not have many cigarettes so he said he preferred to smoke his own. Olivia signaled to Alec and Toby not to argue.

"It's quite true, Doctor Phillipson. My brother-in-law William would love to have Harriet, but unfortunately he has only got two rooms, and he's very much a bachelor. All my relations live in South Africa. We have nowhere to send Harriet or, of course, we would have sent her long ago."

The doctor nodded for he felt sure this was true. The Johnsons were the sort of people who do almost more than is possible for their children.

"It's not doing her any good hanging about by the river at this time of year."

Toby knew how Harriet felt. "What she would like is to go back to school, wouldn't she, Alec?"

Alec was very like his mother; he had some of her elegance and charm, but he had as well a very strongly developed strain of common sense. He could see that Harriet in her daddy-longlegs stage was not really well enough for school.

"That's what she wants, but she's not fit for it, is she?"

"No, she needs to exercise those legs of hers. Do they do gymnasium or dancing at her school?"

"Not really," said Olivia. "Just a little ballroom dancing once a week and physical exercises between classes; you know the sort of thing."

The doctor turned to George. "Would your finances run to sending her to a dancing school or a gymnasium? It would have to be a good one where they knew what they were doing."

George cleared his throat. He hated that kind of question, partly because he was a very proud father who wanted to give his children every advantage, and who, except when he was asked direct questions by doctors, tried to pretend he did give them most advantages.

"I don't think I could manage it now. My father left me a bit, and Olivia will come into quite a lot some day, but just now we're mainly dependent on the shop, and November's a bit of an off-season. You see, my brother William . . ." His voice trailed away.

The doctor, who knew about the shop, felt sorry and filled in the pause by saying "Quite." Then suddenly he had an idea.

"I'll tell you what. How about skating? The manager of the rink nearby is a patient of mine. I'll have a word with him about Harriet. I'm sure he'd let her in for nothing. There'd be the business of the skating shoes, but I believe you can hire those."

Alec nodded. "You can. I think skating's a good idea. If you can get your friend to give her a pass we'll manage the skates."

The doctor got up. "Good. Well, I've got to go and see the manager of the rink tomorrow. I'll have a word with him; if he says yes I'll arrange to pick Harriet up drop her off and introduce her to him. It's no distance; she could have a lot of fun there. Plenty of kids go, I imagine. It's a big, airy place and she can tumble about on the ice and in no time we'll see an improvement in those leg muscles."

George showed the doctor to the door. While he was out of the room Olivia said in a whisper:

"Alec, whatever made you say it would be all right about the skates? What do you suppose they cost?"

Toby answered. "We know what it costs because we went that time Uncle William packed that goose by mistake. They're two shillings a session."

Olivia never lost her air of calm, but she did turn surprised eyes on Alec. He was usually the sensible, reliable one of the family, not at all the sort of person to say they could manage two shillings a day when he knew perfectly well they would be hard put to it to find three pence a day. Alec gave her a reassuring smile.

"It's all right, I'll find it. There's a lot of delivering and stuff will want doing round Christmas, and in the meantime I saw a notice in old Pulton's window. He wants a boy for the paper round."

Olivia flushed. It seemed to her a miserable thing that Harriet's skates had to be earned by her brother instead of by her father and mother. She said:

"I wonder if I could get something to do. I see advertisements for people wanted, but they always seem to be wanted at the same time as I'm wanted here."

Alec laughed. "Don't be silly, Mother. You know as well as I do you couldn't do any more than you do."

Toby had been scowling into space. Now he leaned across to Alec and said:

"How much do you suppose skating shoes cost? If a profit can be made on hiring out a pair of skates at two shillings a session—How much would it cost to buy a second-hand pair outright?"

Alec was doodling on his blotting paper. "With what?" he asked.

At that moment George came back. "Nice fellow, Phillipson. He says this skating will be just the thing for Harriet. It's this skates money that's worrying me. Do you suppose we could do any good if we opened a needlework section, Olivia?"

He was greeted by horrified sounds from Olivia, Alec and Toby. Olivia got up and put her arms round his neck.

"I adore you, George, but you are an impractical old idiot. You haven't yet educated the public to come to you for trout and be prepared at the same time to buy a bag of half-rotten apples, so how do you think you're going to lure them on to supposing they would also like six dusters and a smock?"

Alec looked up from his doodling. "What sort of needle-work did you mean, Dad?"

George looked worried. "Certainly not dusters and smocks. I seem to remember my grandmother doing some very charming things—firescreens, I believe they were."

Olivia laughed. "I'm not much of a needlewoman, and I can promise you even if I were to start today it would be two years before you would have even one firescreen. So I think you can count the needlework department out."

Alec put a bundle of newspapers under the arm of the figure he was doodling. "It's all right, Dad. I'm going to tide us over to start with by a newspaper round. Old Pulton wants somebody."

Toby had been doing some figures on paper. "If a newspaper boy is paid two shillings an hour . . . reckoning one hour in the morning and one hour in the evening daily for six days, with one hour on Sunday at double time, how long would it take him to earn second-hand skates at a cost of five pounds?"

Alec said: "If a boy and a half worked an hour and a half for a skate and a half . . .

Olivia saw Toby felt fun was being made of a serious subject. "I'm afraid, Toby, you're going to grow up to be a financier, one of those people who goes in for big business with a capital B."

Alec finished his drawing. "It wouldn't be a bad thing; We could do with some money in our family. If you were thinking, Toby, that I might get Mr. Pulton to advance five pounds for my services, it wouldn't work—because I might get ill or something and you're too young to be allowed to do it."

"That's right, darling," Olivia agreed. "It wouldn't be practical anyway to buy skating shoes because Harriet's growing, and probably the moment Alec had bought her the shoes they'd be too small. Feet grow terribly fast at her age, especially when you've been ill. I wonder if she's awake?"

George got up. "I'll go and see. If she is I'll bring her down. It'll cheer her up to know what's planned for her."

Harriet was awake, and so was Edward. Edward was the good-looking one; his hair was not sandy like the rest of his family's, but bright copper, and his eyes were enormous with greenish lights in them. Strangers stopped to speak to Edward in the road just because they liked looking at him, and Edward took shameless pleasure in his popularity.

"It's disgusting," Alec often told him. "You're a loathsome show-off."

Edward was always quite unmoved, and merely tried to explain. "I didn't ask to be good-looking, but I like the things being good-looking gives me. I was the prince in the play at school." Toby, when he heard that, had made noises as if he were being sick. "All right, make noises if you like," Edward had said, "but I did like being the prince. There was a special tea afterwards for the actors, with ices."

"But you can't like people cooing and gurgling at you," Toby always protested.

Edward seemed to consider the point. "I don't know. There's you and Alec off to school, and nobody knows you've been, and nobody cares. There's me walks up the same street and everybody knows. I think it's duller to be you."

"It's no good," Alec would say to Toby, "wasting our breath on the little horror."

"Just a born cad," Toby would agree.

But Edward was neither a horror nor a cad, he was just of a very friendly disposition, a person who liked talking and being talked to. Already, although he had only been seven for one month, he had a good idea of the sort of people he liked talking to and the sort of people he did not. He was explaining this to Harriet when George came up to fetch her.

"It's those silly ladies with little dogs I don't like, and people like bus conductors I do like."

George went into Edward's room. "You're supposed to be asleep, my son. Turn over and I'll tuck you in. I'm taking Harriet downstairs."

Edward sat up. "What for? She's supposed to be in bed and asleep too."

George pushed Edward down. "We've got something to tell her." He could feel Edward rising up under his hand to protest that he would like to be told too. "Not tonight, old man. I dare say Harriet'll tell you tomorrow."

If was a cold night, so George not only made Harriet put on her dressing-gown but he rolled her up in an eiderdown and carried her down to the sitting room. Harriet was surprised to find herself downstairs. She looked round at her family with pleasure.

"It's almost worth being sent to bed with Edward to be got up again and brought downstairs. What did Doctor Phillipson say?"

Olivia thought how terribly thin Harriet's face looked sticking out of a bulgy eiderdown. It made her speak very gently.

"He wants you to take up skating, darling."

Nothing could have surprised Harriet more. She had been prepared to hear that she was to go for rides on the top of a bus, or do exercises every morning, but skating was something she had never thought about. George stroked her hair.

"Doctor Phillipson is arranging for you to get in free."

Alec said: "So the only expense will be the hiring of your skates, and that's fixed."

Toby looked hopefully at Harriet for some sign that she was

working out the cost of skates, but Harriet never worked out the cost of anything. She just accepted that there were things you could afford and things you could not.

"When do I start?"

Olivia was thankful Harriet seemed pleased.

"Tomorrow, probably, darling, but you aren't going alone. The doctor's going to take you."

Harriet tried to absorb this strange turn in her affairs. She knew absolutely nothing about skating. Then suddenly a poster for an ice show swam into her mind. The poster had shown a girl in a ballet skirt skating on one foot, the other foot held high above her head, her arms outstretched. Thinking of this picture, Harriet was as startled as if she had been told that tomorrow she would start to be a lion tamer. Could it be possible that she, sitting on her father's knee rolled in an eiderdown, would find herself standing on one leg tomorrow with the foot of the other leg over her head? These thoughts brought her suddenly to more practical matters.

"What do I wear to skate, Mummy?"

Olivia mentally ran a distracted eye over Harriet's wardrobe. She had grown so long in the leg since her illness. There was her school uniform, but that wanted letting down. There were the few frocks made at home. There was the winter party frock cut down from an old dinner dress which had been part of Olivia's trousseau. Dimly Olivia connected skating and dancing.

"I don't know, darling, do you think the brown velvet?"

Harriet thought once more of the poster. "It hasn't got pants that match, and they would show."

"She must match," said Toby. "She'll fall over a lot when she's learning."

Olivia got up. "I must go and get our supper. I think tomorrow, darling, you must just wear your usual skirt and sweater; if you find that's wrong we'll manage something else by the next day."

George stood up and shifted Harriet into a carrying position. "Come up to bed, Miss Sonja Henie."

Harriet's skating ceased to be a serious subject and became funny. Olivia, halfway to the kitchen, turned to laugh.

"My blessed Harriet, what is Daddy calling you? It's only for exercise, darling."

Alec drew a picture of Harriet on his blotting paper: she was flat on her back with her legs in the air. Under it he wrote "Miss Harriet Johnson, Skating Star."

Toby gave Harriet's pigtails a pull. "Queen of the Ice, that's what they'll call you."

George had a big rumbling laugh. "Queen of the Ice! I like that. Queen of the Ice!"

Harriet wriggled. "Don't laugh, Daddy, it tickles."

But when she got back to bed Harriet found that either the laughing or the thought of skating next day had done her good. Her legs were still shaky, but not quite as shaky as they had been before her father had fetched her downstairs. Queen of the Ice! She giggled. The giggle turned into a gurgle. Harriet was asleep.

# CHAPTER 2

## Mr. Pulton

ALEC CALLED ON Mr. Pulton after supper. Mr. Pulton had been born in the flat over the newspaper shop and so had his father before him, and likely enough rows of grandfathers before that. Nobody could imagine a time when Pulton's News Agents had not been a landmark in the High Street. By luck, or because Pulton's did not hold with meddling, the shop still looked as if it had been there a long time. It was a small, low shop with a bowfronted window, and there were the remains of some old bottle glass in one pane. Nobody knew Mr. Pulton's Christian name. He had always been just "Mr. Pulton" to speak to, and "C. Pulton" when he signed his name.

Alec went to Mr. Pulton's back door, as the shop was closed. He knocked loudly because Mr. Pulton was a little deaf. After a moment there was a shuffling, grunting, wheezing sound, and Mr. Pulton opened the door. He was a very thin, very pale man. His hair was white, and so was his face. He wore clothes that nobody had ever seen anyone else wear—a little round brown velvet cap with a tassel hanging down on one side and a brown velvet coat and slippers embroidered with gold and silver thread. His paleness and thinness sticking out of the brown skull cap and the brown velvet coat made him look like a delicate white moth, caught in a rough brown hand. There was nothing delicate or mothlike about Mr. Pulton's mind, however, for that was as quick and as tough as a lizard's. This showed in his extraordinarily blue, shrewd eyes. His voice was misleading for it matched his body and not his mind. It was a tired voice, which sounded as if it had been used such a lot that it was wearing away. As Mr. Pulton looked at Alec, his eyes showed he remembered him and everything that he had heard about him.

"What can I do for you, young man?" he asked.

Alec explained that he had come about the paper round. There was a long pause, not a pause of tiredness but a pause in which Alec could sense Mr. Pulton considering his paper round, and whether Alec was the sort of boy who could be trusted to deliver papers without bringing dishonor to Pulton's News Agents. Evidently his thoughts about Alec were nice, for suddenly he said a very surprising thing.

"Come inside."

Alec had never been inside Mr. Pulton's house before, and neither, as far as he knew, had anybody else. He had often wanted to go inside, because leaning across the counter waiting for his father's paper he had sometimes seen glimpses of a back room, which seemed to be full of interesting things. Now he was inside the room and he found it even more interesting than he had suspected. It was a brownish kind of room, so evidently Mr. Pulton was fond of brown. There were brownish curtains, and brownish chair covers, and brownish walls. There was a gay fire burning, but in spite of it the room was dark because Mr. Pulton had not yet got around to electric light, and could not be bothered with lamps. He lit his home with candles, which gave a queer, dim, flickering light. In spite of the dimness Alec could see that the room was full of pictures, and the pictures were all of horses, which was amazing, for nobody had ever thought of Mr. Pulton as being interested in horses. On the top of a bookcase, on brackets and on tables there were bronze models of horses as well. It seemed such a very horsy sort of room that Alec thought it would not be rude to mention it.

"I say, what a lot of horses, sir."

Mr. Pulton picked up a candle. He walked slowly round his room, and his voice took on a proud, affectionate tone, though it still kept its reedlike quality.

"Old Jenny, foaled a Grand National winner, she did. There he is; his portrait was painted the day after, so my father heard. That's Vinegar, beautiful gray, went to a circus."

He paused by a bronze cast of a horse which was standing on a small table. He ran his hand over the back of the case as if it were alive. "You were a grand horse, weren't you, old fellow? My grandfather's he was; used to hunt with him, he did. My father used to say you were almost human, didn't he? Whisky his name was. Clever, couldn't put a foot wrong."

Alec was so interested in the horses and the little bits of their history that Mr. Pulton let drop, that he forgot the paper round, and it was quite a surprise to him when Mr. Pulton, holding up his candle so that he could see Alec's face clearly, said:

"Why do you want my paper round? Not the type."

"Why not? I'm honest, sober and industrious."

Mr. Pulton chuckled. "Maybe, but you haven't answered my question. Why do you want my paper round?"

Alec, though privately he thought Mr. Pulton was a bit inquisitive, decided he had better explain.

"Well, sir, it's to hire skating shoes for my sister Harriet, who's been ill and . . ."

Mr. Pulton held up a finger to stop Alec.

"Sit down, boy, sit down. At my age you feel your legs, can't keep standing all the time. Besides, I've got my toddy waiting in the fireplace. You like toddy? . . . No, 'course you wouldn't. If you go through that door into my kitchen, and open the cupboard, you'll see in the left-hand corner a bottle marked 'Ginger-wine.' Nothing like ginger-wine for keeping out the cold."

Alec went into the kitchen. It was a very neat, tidy kitchen; evidently whoever looked after Mr. Pulton did it nicely. He found the cupboard easily, and he brought the bottle of ginger-wine and a glass back to the sitting room. Mr. Pulton nodded in a pleased way, and pointed to the chair opposite his own.

"Sit down, boy . . . sit down . . . help yourself. Now tell me about your sister Harriet."

Mr. Pulton was an easy man to talk to. He sat sipping his toddy, now and again nodding his head, and all the time his interested blue eyes were fixed on Alec. When Alec had told him everything, he put down his glass of toddy, folded his hands, and put on the business face he wore in his paper shop.

"How much does it cost to hire skates?"

"Two shillings a session."

Mr. Pulton gave an approving grunt, and shook himself a little as if he were pleased about something.

"Morning and evening rounds. Good. The last boy I had would only do mornings. No good in that never get into my ways. I pay ten shillings a week for the morning round, and four shillings for the evening round. There's not so much work in the evenings; mostly the people buy their papers from a newsboy on the street. . . . You can have the job."

Alec was reckoning the money in his head. Harriet would only go to one session of skating a day six days a week. There would be no skating on Sunday, so it would cost twelve shillings; That would give him two shillings over for himself. Two shillings a week! Because of Uncle William's irregular supplies to the shop, it was scarcely ever that Alec or Toby had any pocket money, and the thought of having two whole shillings a week made Alec's eyes shine brighter than Mr. Pulton's candles.

"Thank you, sir. When can I start?" he asked.

"Tomorrow. You said your sister was starting skating tomorrow. You'll be here at seven and you'll meet my present paper boy; he'll show you round. You look pleased. Think you'll like delivering papers?"

Alec felt warm inside from ginger-wine, and outside from the fire, and being warm inside and out gives one a talkative feeling. Now he said:

"It's the two shillings. You see, Harriet will only need twelve shillings for her skates, and you said fourteen."

Mr. Pulton had picked up his hot toddy again. "That's right. What are you going to do with the other two shillings?"

Ordinarily Alec would not have discussed his secret plan. The only other person who knew it was Toby. But telling things to Mr. Pulton was like telling things to a person in a dream; besides, nobody had ever heard Mr. Pulton discuss somebody else's affairs. Indeed, it was most unlikely that he was interested in anybody's affairs but his own.

"I've no brains," Alec confided. "Toby has those, but Dad and Mother think I'll go on at school until I'm eighteen. But I won't! It's a waste of time for me, at least that's what I think. I'd meant to leave school when I was sixteen, and go into something in Dad's line of business. You see, it's absolutely idiotic our depending on Uncle William. Dad doesn't see that, but of course he wouldn't for he's his brother. But you can't really make a place pay when for days on end you get nothing but rhubarb and perhaps a couple of rabbits, and one boiling hen, and then suddenly thousands of old potatoes. You see, Uncle William just rushes out and sends off things he doesn't like the look of, or has got too many of. Now what I want to do is to get a proper setup. I'd like a pony and cart to go to market and buy the sort of things customers want to eat. What we sell now, and everybody knows it, isn't what customers want but what Uncle William doesn't want. I think knowing that puts people off buying from Dad."

Mr. Pulton leaned back in his chair. "It'd take a lot of two shillings to buy a pony and trap."

"I know, but I might be able to do something as a start. You see, if I put all the two shillings together, by next spring I'd have a little capital and I could at least try stocking Dad with early potatoes or something of that sort. We never sell new potatoes—Uncle William likes those, so we only get the old ones. If the potatoes went well I might be able to buy peas, beans, strawberries and raspberries in the summer."

You never have those either?

"Of course not, Uncle William hogs the lot."

"You'd like to own a grocery store some day?" Mr. Pulton asked.

"Glory no! I'd hate it. What I want is to be at the growing end. I'd give anything to have the sort of setup Uncle William's got. There's a decent-sized walled fruit-and-vegetable garden, where you could do pretty well if you went in for cloches, and there's a nice bit of river and there's some rough shooting."

"How does your Uncle William send his produce to your father?"

Alec looked as exasperated as he felt. "That's another idiotic thing. We never know how it's coming. Sometimes he has a friend with a car, and we get a telephone message, and Dad has to run up to somebody's flat to fetch it. Mostly it comes by train, but sometimes Uncle William gets a bargee to bring it down; that's simply awful because the stuff arrives bad, and Uncle William can't understand that it arrived bad."

Mr. Pulton had finished his toddy, and he got up. "I am going to bed. Don't forget now, seven o'clock in the morning. Not a minute late. I can't abide boys who come late." He was turning to go when evidently a thought struck him. He nodded in a pleased sort of way. "Stick to your dreams, don't let anyone put you off what you want to do. All these"—he swept his hand round the horses—"were my grandfather's and my great grandfather's. Just that hunter belonged to my father. When I was your age I dreamed of horses, but there was this news agency; there's always been a Pulton in this shop. Where are my dreams now? Good night, boy."

# CHAPTER 3

# The Rink

OLIVIA WENT TO the rink with Harriet, for the more Harriet thought about the girl on the poster, standing on one skate with the other foot high over her head, the more sure she was that she would be too shy to go alone to a place where people could do things like that. Doctor Phillipson was very kind, but he was a busy, rushing, tearing sort of man, who would be almost certain to introduce her to the manager by just saying "This is Harriet," and then dash off again.

This was exactly what happened. Doctor Phillipson called for Harriet and her mother just after lunch and took them to the rink. He hurried them into a small office in which was a tired, busy-looking man said, "This is Harriet, and her mother, Mrs. Johnson. Harriet, this is Mr. Matthews, the manager of the rink. I've got a patient to see," and he was gone.

It took no time for Olivia to make friends with Mr. Matthews. She heard all about something called his duodenal ulcer, which was why he knew Doctor Phillipson, and all about how Doctor Phillipson had taken out his wife's appendix, and of how Doctor Phillipson had looked after his twin boys, who were grown up now and married. Only when there were no more illnesses in the Matthews' family left to talk about did Olivia mention skating.

"Doctor Phillipson tells me you're going to be very kind and let Harriet come here to skate. He wants her to have exercise for her leg muscles."

Mr. Matthews looked at Harriet's legs in a worried sort of way. "Thin, aren't they? Ever skated before?" Harriet explained she had not. "Soon pick it up. I'll show you where you go for your skating shoes. Cost two shillings a session, they will." He turned to Olivia. "I'll have a word with my man who hires them out, ask him to find a pair that fit her. He'll keep them for her; it'll make all the difference."

The way to the skate-hiring place was through the rink. Harriet had never seen a rink before. She gazed with her eyes open very wide at what seemed to her an enormous room with ice for a floor. In the middle of the ice were people—many of whom did not look any older than she was—doing what seemed to her terribly difficult things with their legs. On the outside of the rink, however, there were a comforting lot of people who seemed to know as little about skating as she did. They were holding onto the barrier round the side of the rink as if it was their only hope of keeping alive, while their legs did the most curious things in a way that evidently surprised their owners. In spite of holding onto the barrier, a lot of these skaters fell down and seemed to find it terribly difficult to get up again.

Harriet slipped her hand into her mother's and pulled her down so that she could speak to her quietly without Mr. Matthews' hearing.

"It doesn't seem to matter here, not being able to skate, does it, Mummy?"

Olivia knew just how Harriet was feeling. "Of course not,

pet. Perhaps some day you'll be as grand a skater as those children in the middle."

Mr. Matthews overheard what Olivia said. "I don't know so much about that. Takes time and money to become a fine skater. See that little girl there?"

Harriet followed the direction in which Mr. Matthews was pointing, and saw a girl of about her own age. She was a very grand-looking little girl wearing a white sweater, a short white pleated skirt, white tights, white shoes, and a small white tight-fitting bonnet. She was a dark child with lots of loose curly hair and big dark eyes.

"The little girl in white?" Harriet asked.

"That's right. Little Lalla Moore, promising child. Been brought here for a lesson almost every day since she was three."

Olivia looked pityingly at Lalla. "Poor little creature! I can't imagine she wanted to come here when she was three."

Mr. Matthews obviously thought that coming to his rink at the age of three brought credit on the rink, for his voice sounded proud. "Pushed here in a pram, she was, by her nanny."

"I wonder," said Olivia, "what could have made her parents think she wanted to skate when she was three."

Mr. Matthews started walking again towards the skate-hiring place. "It's not her parents—they were both killed skating. Been brought up by an aunt. Her father was Cyril Moore."

Mr. Matthews said "Cyril Moore" in so important a voice that it was obvious he thought Olivia ought to know whom he was talking about. Olivia had never heard of anybody called Cyril Moore, but she said in a surprised, pleased tone:

"Cyril Moore! Fancy!"

At the skate-hiring place Mr. Matthews introduced Olivia and Harriet to the man in charge.

"This is Sam. Sam, I want you to look after this little girl. Her name is Harriet Johnson, she's a friend of Doctor Phillipson's, and as you can see from the look of her, she has been ill. Find shoes that fit her and keep them for her. She'll be coming every day."

Sam was a cheerful, red-faced man. As soon as Mr. Matthews had gone he pulled forward a chair.

"Sit down, duckie, and let's have a dekko at those feet." He ran a hand up and down Harriet's calves and made disapproving, clicking sounds. "My, my! Putty, not muscles, these are."

Harriet did not want Sam to think she had been born with flabby legs. She said:

"They weren't always like this. It's because they've been in bed so long with nothing to do. It seems to have made them feel terribly shaky, but Doctor Phillipson thinks if I skate they'll get all right again. I feel rather despondent about them myself. They've been shaky a long time."

Sam took one of Harriet's hands, closed it into a fist and banked it against his right leg.

"What about that? That's my spare, that is—the Japs had the other in Burma. Do you think it worries me? Not a bit of it. You'd be surprised what I can do with me old spare. I reckon I get around more with one whole leg and one spare than most do with two whole legs. Don't you lose 'eart in yours; time we've had you on the rink a week or two you'll have forgotten they ever felt shaky. Proper little skater's legs they'll be."

"Like Lalla Moore's?" Harriet asked.

Sam looked surprised. "Know her?"

"No, but Mr. Matthews showed her to us. He said she'd been skating since she was three. He said she used to come in a perambulator."

Sam turned as if to go into his shop, then he stopped.

"So she did, too. Had proper little shoes made for her and all. I often wonder what her Dad would say if he could come back and see what they were doing to his kid. Cyril Moore he was—one of the best figure skaters, and one of the nicest men I ever set eyes on. Well, mustn't stay gossiping here, you want to get on the ice."

"Mummy, isn't he nice?" Harriet whispered. "I should think he's a knowing man about legs, wouldn't you? He ought to know about them, having had to get used to having one instead of two."

The shoes that Sam found were new, and had skates attached. He explained that new shoes were stiffer and therefore would be a better support for Harriet's thin ankles. Sam seemed so proud of having found her a pair of shoes that were new and a fairly good fit that Harriet tried to pretend she thought they were lovely. Actually she thought they were awful. Lalla Moore's beautiful white skating shoes had made Harriet hope she was going to wear white shoes too, but the ones Sam put on her were a nasty shade of brown, with a band of green painted round the edge of the soles. Sam was not deceived by her trying to look pleased.

" 'Ired shoes is all right, but nobody can't say they're oil paintings. If you want them stylish white ones you'll have to buy your own. We buy for hard wear—you'd be surprised the time we make our shoes last. Besides, nobody can't make off with these."

Olivia looked puzzled. "Does anyone want to?"

"You'd be surprised, but they don't get away with it. If Harriet here was to walk out with these someone would spot the green paint and be after her quicker than you could say winkle."

Olivia laughed. "I can't see Harriet walking out in these. I'm going to have a job to get her to the rink."

Sam finished lacing Harriet's skates. He gave the right one an affectionate pat.

"Too right you will. I wasn't speaking personal, I was just

explaining why the shoes look the way they do." He got up. "Good luck, duckie, enjoy yourself."

If Olivia had not been there to hold her up, Harriet would never have reached the rink. Her feet rolled over first to the right, and then to the left. She clung to Olivia, and then lurched over and clung to a wall. When she came to some stairs that led to the rink it seemed to her as if she would be killed trying to get down them. The skates had behaved badly on the flat floor, but walking downstairs they behaved as if they had gone mad. She reached the bottom by gripping the stair rail with both hands while Olivia held her round her waist, lifting her so that her skates hardly touched the stairs. Olivia was breathless but triumphant when they got to the edge of the rink.

"Off you go now! I'll sit here and get my breath back."

Harriet gazed in horror at the ice. The creepers and crawlers who were beginners like herself clung so desperately to the barrier that she could not see much room to get in between them. Another thing was that even if she could find a space, it was almost certain that one of the creepers and crawlers in front or behind her would choose that moment to fall over and knock her down at the same time. As a final terror, between the grand skaters in the middle of the rink and the creepers and crawlers round the edge, there were rough people. They seemed to go round and round like express trains, their chins stuck forward, their hands behind their backs, with apparently no other object than to see how fast they could go, and they did not seem to mind whom they knocked over as they went.

Gripping both sides of an opening in the barrier, Harriet put one foot towards the ice and hurriedly took it back. This happened five times.

Olivia was sympathetic but firm. "I'm sorry, darling, I'd be scared stiff myself, but it's no good wasting all the afternoon holding onto the barrier and never getting on the ice. Be brave and take the plunge."

Harriet looked as desperate as she felt. "Do you think I'd feel braver if I shut my eyes?"

"No, darling, I think that would be fatal. Someone would be bound to knock you down."

It was at that moment that Olivia felt a tap on her shoulder. She turned round. Behind her sat an elderly lady in a bulgy gray suit. On her head she wore a neat black straw hat, and she was knitting a white woolen sweater.

"If you'll wait a moment, ma'am, I'll signal to my little girl. She'll take her onto the ice for you."

"Isn't that kind!" said Olivia. "Which is your little girl?"

The lady stood up. Standing up she was even bulgier than she had been when she was sitting down. She waved her knitting.

"She's not mine really. I'm her nurse."

From the center of the ring the waving was answered. Harriet nudged her mother.

"Lalla Moore!"

Lalla cared nothing for people who went round pretending they were express trains, or for creepers and crawlers. She came flying across the rink as if she were running across an empty field.

"What is it, Nana?" she asked.

"This little girl, dear." Nana turned to Harriet. "You haven't been on the ice before, have you, dear?"

Harriet was gazing at Lalla. "No, and I don't really want to now. The doctor says I've got to. It's to stop my legs from feeling like cotton wool."

Nana looked at Harriet's legs with an I-thought-as-much expression.

"Take her carefully, Lalla, and don't let her fall."

Lalla took hold of Harriet's hands. She moved backwards. Suddenly Harriet found she was on the ice.

"You'll have to try and straighten your legs a little, because then I can tow you," Lalla told her.

Harriet's knees and ankles hadn't been very good at standing straight on an ordinary floor since she had been ill, and in skates it was even more difficult. But Lalla had been skating for so long she could not see anything difficult about standing up on skates, and because of that Harriet began to believe it could not be as hard as it looked. Presently Lalla, skating backwards, had towed her into the center of the rink.

"There, now I'll show you how to start. Spread your feet apart." With great difficulty Harriet got her feet into the position that Lalla wanted. "Now lift them up. First your right foot. Put it down on the ice. Now your left foot. Put it down."

Nana, having asked Olivia's permission to do so, had moved into the seat next to her. First of all they discussed Harriet's illness and her leg muscles. Then Olivia said:

"Mr. Matthews pointed out your child to us. I hear she's been skating since she was a baby; you used to push her here in a perambulator, didn't you?"

Nana laid her knitting in her lap. She could tell from Olivia's tone that she thought it odd teaching a baby to skate.

"So I did too, and I didn't like it. I never have held with fancy upbringing for my children, and I never will.

"But her father was a great skater, wasn't he?"

"He was Cyril Moore. And maybe your father was a great preacher, ma'am, but that isn't to say you want to spend all your life preaching."

Olivia laughed. "My father has a citrus estate in South

Africa, and I've certainly never wanted to spend my life growing oranges and lemons."

"Nor would her father have wanted skating for Lalla as a baby. Bless him, he was a lovely gentleman and so was her mother a lovely lady."

"What happened to them?" Olivia asked.

"Well, he was the kind of gentleman that must always be doing something dangerous. He only had to see a board up saying 'Don't skate, danger' and he was on the ice in a minute. That's how he went, and poor Mrs. Moore with him. Seems he was on a pond; they say there was a warning out the ice wouldn't bear, but anyway they both popped through it, and were never seen alive again."

"Oh dear, what a sad story. And who is bringing little Lalla up?"

Nana's voice took on a reserved tone. "Her Aunt Claudia, her father's only sister."

"And she was the one who decided to make a skater of her?"

"It's a memorial, so she says. Lalla wasn't two years old the winter her parents popped through that thin ice. I'll never forget it. Her Aunt Claudia moved into the house, and the very first thing she did was to have a glass case made for the skates Lalla's father was drowned in. She put it up over my blessed lamb's cot. 'With all respect, ma'am,' I said, 'I don't think it's wholesome. We don't want her growing up to brood on what's happened.' And do you know what she said? 'He's to live again in Lalla, Nana. He was a wonderful skater, but Lalla is to be the greatest skater in the world.'"

Olivia, enthralled with the story, had forgotten about Harriet. She turned now to look at the two children.

"I don't know whether she's going to be the greatest skater in the world, but she certainly seems to be a wonderful teacher. Look at my Harriet."

Nana was silent a moment watching the two children. Then, "We'll call them back in a minute. Harriet shouldn't be at it too long, not the first time. They say Lalla's coming on wonderfully. She's got her bronze medal, you know, and she won't be ten for six months."

Olivia had no idea what a bronze medal was for but she could tell from Nana's tone it was something important.

"Isn't that splendid!"

"It's a funny life for a child, and not what I expect in my nurseries. She has to do so much time on the ice every day that she can't go to school or anything like that. Governesses and tutors she has, as well as being coached here every day, of course, by Mr. Lindblom."

"It must cost a terrible lot of money."

"Well, what with the money her parents left her, and her Aunt Claudia marrying a rich man, there's enough."

"She has an uncle, has she?" asked Olivia.

Nana was knitting again; she smiled at the wool in a pleased way. "Yes, indeed. Her Uncle David. Mr. David King he is, and as nice a gentleman as you could wish to find. I couldn't ask for better."

Olivia was glad to hear that Lalla had a nice uncle because somehow, from the tone of Nana's voice, she was not certain she would like Lalla's Aunt Claudia. However, it was not fair to make up her mind about somebody she had never met, and anyway probably Lalla enjoyed the skating.

"I expect the skating's fun for her, even if she has to miss school and have governesses and tutors because of it."

"She enjoys it well enough, bless her, I'm not saying she

doesn't; but it's not what I would choose, in. a manner of speaking." Nana got up. "I'm going to signal the children to come off the ice, for if you don't mind my mentioning it, your little Harriet has done more than enough for the time being. She'd better sit down, beside me and have a sweet the same as I give my Lalla."

The moment she sat down Harriet found her legs were much more wobbly than they had been before. They felt so tired she did not know where to put them, and kept wriggling about. Nana noticed this.

"You'll get used to it, dearie. Everybody's legs get tired at first."

Olivia looked anxiously at Harriet. "Perhaps that had better be all for today, darling."

Harriet was shocked at the suggestion. "Mummy! Two whole shillings' worth of hired skates used up in a quarter of an hour! We couldn't, we simply couldn't."

"It can't be helped if you're tired, darling. It's better to waste part of the two shillings than to wear the poor legs out altogether." Olivia turned to Nana. "I'm sure you agree with me."

Nana had a cozy way of speaking, which sounded as if while she was about nothing could ever go very wrong.

"That's right, ma'am. More haste less speed, so I've always said in my nurseries." She smiled at Harriet. "You sit down and have another sweet and presently Lalla will take you on the ice for another five minutes. That'll be enough for the first day."

Lalla looked pleadingly at Nana. "Could I, oh could I stay and talk to Harriet, Nana?"

Nana looked up from her knitting. "It'll mean making the time up afterwards. You know Mr. Lindblom said you was to work at your eight-foot one."

Lalla laughed. "One-foot eight, Nana." She turned to Harriet. "Nana never gets the names of the figures right."

Nana was quite unmoved by this criticism. "Nor any reason why I should, never having taken up ice skating nor having had the wish."

"Harriet would never have taken up ice skating, not had the wish either," said Olivia, "if it hadn't been for her legs. I believe two of my sons came here once, but that's as near as the Johnsons have ever got to skating."

Lalla was staring at Olivia with round eyes. "Two of your sons! Has Harriet got brothers?" Harriet explained about Alec, Toby and Edward, and Lalla sighed with envy. "Lucky, lucky you. Three brothers! Imagine, Nana! I'd rather have three brothers than anything else in the world."

Nana turned her knitting round and started another row. "No good wishing. If you were to have three brothers, you'd have to do without a lot of things you take for granted now."

"I wouldn't mind. I wouldn't mind anything. You know, Harriet, it's simply awful being only one. There's nobody to play with."

Olivia felt sorry for Lalla. "Perhaps, Nana, you would bring her to the house sometime to play with Harriet and the boys. It isn't a big house, and there are a lot of us in it, but we'd love to have her and you too, of course."

"Bigness isn't everything," said Nana. "Some day, if the time could be made, it would be a great treat."

Harriet looked with respect at Lalla. Even when she had gone to school she had always had time to do things. She could not imagine a life when you had to make time to go out to tea. Lalla saw Harriet's expression and explained:

"It's awful how little time I get. I do lessons in the morning, then there is a special class for dancing or fencing. Then, directly after lunch, we come here—and with my lesson and the things I have to practice, I'm always here two hours and sometimes three. By the time I get home and have had tea it's almost bedtime."

Olivia thought this a very sad description of the day for someone who was not yet ten.

"There must be time for a game or something before bedtime, isn't there? Don't you play games with your aunt?"

Lalla looked surprised at the question. "Oh no, she doesn't play my sort of games. She goes out and plays bridge and things like that. When I see her we talk about skating, nothing else."

"She's very interested in how Lalla's getting on," Nana explained. "But Lalla and I have a nice time before she goes to bed, don't we, dear? Sometimes we listen to the wireless, and sometimes, when Uncle David and Aunt Claudia are out, we go downstairs and look at that television."

Olivia tried to think of something to say, but she couldn't. It seemed to her a miserable description of Lalla's evenings. Nana was a darling, but how much more fun it would be for Lalla if she could have somebody of her own age to play with. She was saved answering by Lalla.

"Are your legs better enough now to come on the rink, Harriet?"

Harriet stretched out first one leg and then the other to see how wobbly they were. They were still a bit feeble, but she was not going to disgrace herself in front of Lalla by saying so. She tottered up onto her skates. Lalla held out her hands. "I'll take you to the middle of the rink, but this time you'll have to lift up your feet by yourself—I'm not going to hold you. Don't mind if you fall down. It doesn't hurt much."

Olivia watched Harriet's unsteady progress to the middle of the rink.

"How lucky for her that she met Lalla! It would have taken

her weeks to have got a few inches round the edge by herself. She's terrified, poor child, but she won't dare show it in front of Lalla."

Nana went on knitting busily. Her voice showed that she was not quite sure she ought to say what she was saying. "When I get the chance I'll have a word with Mrs. King about Harriet, or maybe with Mr. King. He's the one for seeing things reasonably. It would be a wonderful thing for Lalla if you would allow Harriet to come back to tea sometimes after the skating. It would be such a treat for her to have someone to play with."

"Harriet would love it, but I am afraid it is out of the question for some time yet. I'm afraid coming here and walking home will be about all she can manage. The extra walk to and from your house would be too much for her at present," Olivia replied.

"There wouldn't be any walking. We'd send her home in the car. Mrs. King drives her own nearly always, and Mr. King his own, so the chauffeur's got nothing to do except drive Lalla about in the little car."

Olivia laughed. "How very grand! I'm afraid I'll never be able to ask you to our house. Three cars and a chauffeur! I'm certain Mrs. King would have a fit if she saw how we lived."

"Lot of foolishness. Harriet's a nice little girl, and just the friend for Lalla. You leave it to me. Mrs. King has her days, and I'll pick a good one before I speak of Harriet to her or Mr. King."

Walking home, Olivia asked Harriet how she had enjoyed skating. She noticed with happiness that Harriet was looking less like a daddy-longlegs than she had since her illness started.

"It was gorgeous, Mummy, but of course it was made gorgeous by Lalla. I do like her. I hope her Aunt Claudia will let me go to tea. Lalla's afraid she won't, and she's certain she won't let her come to tea with us."

"You never know. Nana says she has her days, and she's going to try telling her about you on one of her good days."

Harriet said nothing for a moment. She was thinking about
Lalla, Nana and Aunt Claudia, and mixed up with thinking of
them was thinking about telling her father, Alec, Toby and Edward about them. Suddenly she stood still.

"Mummy, mustn't it be simply awful to be Lalla? Imagine
going home every day with no one to talk to except Nana, and she
knows what's happened because she was there all the time. Don't
you think that to be the only one, like Lalla, is the most awful
thing that could happen to anybody?"

Olivia thought of the three cars and the chauffeur, and
Lalla's lovely clothes, and of the queer food the Johnsons had to
eat at home and the shop that never paid. Then she thought of
George and the boys, and the fun of hearing about Alec's first day
on the paper round, and how everybody would want to know
about Harriet's afternoon at the rink. Perhaps it was nicer to laugh
till you were almost sick over the shop-leavings you had to eat
than to have the grandest dinner in the world served in lonely
state to two people in a nursery. She squeezed Harriet's hand.

"Awful. Poor Lalla, we must make a vow, Harriet. Aunt
Claudia or no Aunt Claudia, let's make friends with Lalla."

CHAPTER 4

Lalla's House

LALLA'S HOUSE WAS the exact opposite of Harriet's house. It was not far away, but in a much grander neighborhood. It was a charming, low white house lying back in a big garden, with sloping lawns leading down to the river. Where the lawn and the river joined there was a little landing stage to which Lalla's Uncle David kept his motor launch tied in the summer.

Lalla's rooms were at the top of the house. A large room overlooking the river, which had been her nursery, was now her schoolroom, and another big room next to it was her bedroom. There was a room for Nana and a bathroom as well. Her bedroom was the sort of bedroom that most girls of her age would like to have. The carpet was blue and the bedspread and curtains white printed with wreaths of pink roses tied with blue ribbons, and there was a frill of the same material round her dressing-table.

The only ugly thing in the room was the glass case over her bed in which the skating shoes in which her father was drowned were kept. The nicest skating shoes in the world are not ornamental, and these, although they had been polished, looked as though someone had been drowned in them, for the black leather had got a brownish-green look. Underneath the case was a plaque which

Aunt Claudia had put up. It had the name of Lalla's father on it, the date on which he was born and the date on which he was drowned and, underneath, that he was the world's champion figure skater. Above the case Aunt Claudia had put some words from the Bible: "Go, and do thou likewise." This made people smile, for it sounded rather as if Aunt Claudia meant Lalla to be drowned. Lalla did not care whether anybody smiled at the glass case or not, for she thought it idiotic keeping old skates in a glass case, and knew from what Nana had told her that her father and mother would have thought it idiotic; in fact she was sure everybody thought it idiotic except Aunt Claudia.

The schoolroom, which Lalla sometimes forgot to call the schoolroom and called the nursery, was another very pretty room. It had a blue carpet and blue walls, lemon yellow curtains and lemon yellow seats on the chairs, and yellow cushions on the window seats. It still had nursery things like Lalla's rocking horse and dolls' house, and a toy cupboard simply bulging with toys, but it also had low bookcases, full of books, pretty china ornaments, good pictures and a radio. The only things which did not go with the room were on a shelf which ran all down one wall. This was full of the silver trophies that Lalla's father had won.

It is a very nice thing to win silver trophies, but a great many of them all together do not look pretty. The only time Lalla liked the trophies was at Christmas, because then she filled them with holly and they looked gay. Although every trophy and medal had her father's name on it, where he had won it, what for, and the date on which it had been won, Aunt Claudia was afraid Lalla might forget to read the inscriptions. This was sensible of her because Lalla certainly would not have read them, so underneath the whole length of the shelf was a quotation from Sir Walter Scott altered by Aunt Claudia to suit a girl by changing "his" and "him" into "her": "Her square-turn'd joints and strength of limb, Show'd her no carpet knight so trim, But in close fight a champion grim."

When Aunt Claudia came to the nursery she would sometimes read the lines out loud in a very grand acting way. She hoped hearing them said like that would inspire Lalla to further effort, but all it did was to make Lalla decide that she would never read any book by Sir Walter Scott. Sometimes Lalla and Nana had a little joke about the verse; Lalla would jump out of her bed or her bath and fling herself on Nana saying "Her square-turn'd joints and strength of limb"—and then butt Nana with her head and say, "That butt never came from a carpet knight, did it?"

On the day that Lalla met Harriet she and Nana had an exceptionally gay tea. Nana had let Lalla do what she loved doing, which was kneel by the fire making her own toast instead of having it sent up hot and buttered from the kitchen. They talked about Harriet and the rink, Lalla in an excited way and Nana rather cautiously. Lalla laughed at Nana and said she was being "mimsy-pimsy" and asked if it was because she didn't like the Johnsons. Nana shook her head.

"I liked them very much, dear. Mrs. Johnson's a real lady, as anyone can see, and little Harriet, for all she's so shabby, has been brought up as a little lady should. But I don't want you to go fixing your heart on having her here. You know what it is—your Aunt Claudia has got strict ideas of who you should know. And I don't think if she was to see Harriet she would think Harriet was your sort, not having the money to live as you do." Nana could see this was going to make Lalla angry, so she added: "Now don't answer back, dear, you know I'm speaking sense. I don't think it matters about what money a person has, no more than you do, but your aunt's your guardian, and she sets great store by money.

You know you've been brought up never to want for anything, so you must be a good girl and not mind too much if you're not allowed to have Harriet here."

"But I want to go to Harriet's house. I want to be in a family."

"I dare say, but maybe 'want' will have to be your master. The one that pays the piper calls the tune, and the piping in this house is done by your Aunt Claudia, and you know it."

Nana had only just finished saying this when the door opened and Aunt Claudia walked in. Nana was swallowing a sip of tea, and she was so upset at Aunt Claudia's having so narrowly missed hearing what she had said that she choked. Lalla thought this funny and began to giggle. Aunt Claudia did not like either choking or giggling, and her voice sounded as though she did not.

Aunt Claudia was a very nice-looking woman in a hard sort of way. She had fair hair that looked as if it had been gummed into place, because there was never one hair out of order. Her face was always beautifully made up, so that cold winds, hot weather, even colds in the head never made any difference to it. She wore beautiful clothes and lovely jewels. Although she felt annoyed to find Nana choking and Lalla giggling, she did not let it show on her face, because she knew that made wrinkles. The only place where it showed was in her blue eyes, which had a sparkish look.

"Good evening, Nurse. Can't you control that noise? Lalla, I don't think you should find it funny when Nurse is choking." She waited till Nana's last choke died away, and Lalla had stifled her giggles. "I don't seem to have seen you all the week, and I've got a few minutes before I go out, so I thought I'd hear how your skating is progressing. Have you mastered the one-foot eight?"

Lalla was not being very quick at the one-foot figure eight because she was not trying hard enough.

"It's not right yet, at least not right enough for Mr. Lindblom, but I'm working at it, aren't I, Nana?"

Nana was glad that after Harriet had gone she had sent Lalla back to work at that figure. It would have been difficult for her to sound convincing if what she could remember was Lalla's holding up Harriet while Harriet lifted first one foot and then the other off the ice.

"She worked nicely today, ma'am. I'm sure you would be pleased with her."

Aunt Claudia pulled up an armchair to the fire and sat down. "Why today? Surely every day. You are so lucky, Lalla. How many thousands of girls throughout the country would envy you your opportunities to learn, and your gift?"

Lalla had heard this kind of thing so often that it went in one ear and out the other. "They're awfully difficult figures for the inter-silver."

Aunt Claudia beckoned to her. Lalla came to her unwillingly. Aunt Claudia drew her down to sit on the arm of her chair. "That's not the eager face I like to see. I know you don't care for figure skating as much as you do for free skating, but you know as well as I do that you've got to know all these figures to perfection before you can become world champion."

Lalla wriggled. "Suppose I never was a world champion. It would seem mean to have spent such ages learning figures."

Aunt Claudia forgot her, make-up and frowned. Her voice was severe.

"Lalla! You know I don't like that kind of talk. You will be a world champion. Already you're the most gifted child in the country. I know that in your heart of hearts you live for nothing else but your skating, but sometimes you say things which hurt me very much. You are dedicated to follow in your father's footsteps and you know it." She raised her eyes to the silver cups. Lalla, knowing what was coming, looked over her shoulder at Nana and made a face. Aunt Claudia took a deep breath and raised her voice: "'Her square-turn'd joints and strength of limb, Show'd her no carpet knight so trim, But in close fight a champion grim.'" Nana's reverent "And very nice too, ma'am," sounded almost like Amen.

Aunt Claudia got up and shook out her skirts.

"Well, I must be going to my party." She held Lalla's hand and led her towards the door. At the door she turned and pointed again to the cups. "Cyril Moore's daughter. Lalla Moore, world champion. We'll make his name live again, won't we, dear? Good night. Good night, Nurse."

After Aunt Claudia had gone Lalla came back to the table to finish her tea, but it wasn't a gay tea any more. Nana saw Lalla was playing about with her toast.

"It's no good worrying, dear. You can only do the best you can."

Lalla stabbed at her toast with her knife. "You say that because nobody thought when you were nearly ten that you had got to be a world champion at anything."

Nana thought back to her childhood. She saw herself and her eight brothers and sisters sitting round the table at the lodge of the big house where her father was gardener. In her memory she heard him say as he had said very often when she was little: "I don't mind what work any of you do as long as you have your feet under somebody else's table." This meant they should take jobs where their homes were provided, and their breakfast, dinner, lunch and tea, so that all the money they earned, even if it was not very much, was free to be spent on other things besides living. Nana remembered the cozy feeling it had given her when her father had said that, because she had always meant to go into service and work in a nursery, so what her father wanted she wanted, and nothing could have been nicer.

Nana was sorry for Lalla; she thought it must be terrible to have to be the best woman skater in the world, and sometimes trembled to think what would happen if Lalla did not manage to be it. Lalla loved skating when she could do what she liked, but Mr. Lindblom often had to scold her about the way she did figures, and sometimes Nana had heard him say: "You are not trying, Lalla. You could do it if you worked." Every time he said things like that Nana's heart gave a jump, and she thought how lucky it was that Aunt Claudia was not at the rink to hear him. She got up.

"I'll clear the tea table. What are you going to do till bedtime? That jigsaw puzzle?"

Lalla turned on the radio, but there was nothing that she was in the mood to hear, so she turned it off again and wandered out into the passage, feeling cross and loose-endish. She hung over the banisters and watched Aunt Claudia go downstairs dressed for a party. She admired Aunt Claudia's clothes very much and thought how nice it would be to be grown up, going to parties whenever you liked, wearing a mink coat. She heard Aunt Claudia speak to the parlormaid: "Tell Mr. King I did wait, will you, Wilson, but I went on without him; and will he please follow me. He knows where the party is."

Wilson said "Yes, ma'am," opened the front door and then shut it.

Lalla liked Wilson, so she slid down the banisters to her on her tummy. Wilson watched her arrive and made clicking, disapproving sounds.

"If I was your Nana I'd take a strap to you if I saw you doing that. Look at the front of your white sweater!"

Lalla put her arm through Wilson's. "Do you think Uncle David's going to the party?"

Wilson's eyes twinkled. "Not if he can help it, he won't. You know what he thinks of them." She lowered her voice. "I didn't say so to your aunty, but when he was going out this morning he said to me, 'I think I shall be kept at work tonight, Wilson, so I'll be too late to go to the party Mrs. King's going to. You'd better put drinks in my study.'"

Lalla gave a pleased skip. "Good. I shall come down and talk to him."

On the days when Aunt Claudia was out alone, Lalla often came down and talked to her uncle. Uncle David was a long, thin man with dark hair and blue eyes. He had always wanted to have a daughter, so he was pleased that Aunt Claudia had a girl ward. From the very beginning he had been fond of Lalla, and as she grew older and became more of a companion, he got fonder still. But he had to keep what friends he and Lalla were a secret from Aunt Claudia, for from Aunt Claudia's point of view he was not a suitable friend for Lalla, because he had a great failing. No matter how often Aunt Claudia explained to him about Lalla's father, nor how often she repeated to him the praise and nice things people at the rink said about Lalla, she could not make him take Lalla's skating seriously. He was the sort of man who thought skating, like other sports, was a lovely hobby, but a nuisance when you tried to be first-class at it. Obviously, feeling as she did about skating for Lalla, Aunt Claudia did not like that sort of talk in front of her, so she did not let Lalla see more of her uncle than she could help.

Uncle David was sitting on the leather top of his window seat when Lalla came in. He was pleased to see her.

"How's the seventh wonder of the world this evening?"

Lalla did not mind being teased by Uncle David. She sat down next to him on the seat and told him about her afternoon and how she had met Harriet.

"You can't think how nice she is. She's just the same age as me, but taller, but that's because she's been in bed for months and months, so her legs have got very long. She is so thin." Lalla held up her hands about twelve inches apart. "Even the thickest part of her is not thicker than that, and she's got the most gorgeous mother called Mrs. Johnson and she's got three brothers and a father. Oh, I do envy her. I wish I had three brothers." She looked up anxiously at Uncle David. "I want awfully for her to come to tea with me, and me to go to tea with her. Nana thinks I won't be able to because she isn't rich like we are. Can you think of any way which would make her being poor not matter to Aunt Claudia?"

Uncle David was a sensible sort of man. He never treated Lalla as if she were more silly than a grown-up because she was a child. He lit a cigarette while he thought ever what she had said.

"What's the father?"

Lalla lowered her voice. "Nana doesn't know, but it's some sort of a shop."

Uncle David whispered back: "You and I don't care how anyone earns his living, do we, as long as it's honest? But I don't think your aunt's going to cotton onto a shop."

"I think it's rather an odd sort of shop. Harriet said they only sold things that their Uncle William grew or shot or caught on his land in the country. And that was why they were so poor, because her Uncle William eats a lot so they only get what's left."

Uncle David was gazing at the carpet, as if by looking at it very hard he could see into the past.

"William Johnson. William Johnson. That strikes a note. I suppose Harriet didn't say what her father's Christian name was?"

"It's George. Harriet said that Alec—that's the eldest of her brothers—Alec's real name's George, but he's called Alec because he couldn't have the same first name as his father."

Uncle David got up and began pacing up and down the carpet.

"William and George Johnson. Shiver my timbers, but that strikes a note somewhere." Suddenly he swung round to Lalla. "I have it! You ask your Harriet where her father went to school. There were a couple of brothers at my prep school, William and George. If it's the same we might be able to do something."

Lalla looked puzzled. "Would it make it better that Harriet's father went to the same school as you?"

Uncle David nodded.

"I can't tell you why, but it does." He looked at the clock. "You'd better be skipping, poppet, don't want to blot your copybook by your being caught in here." He gave her a kiss. "I like the sound of your Harriet; I'll have a word with Nana about her, and if it's the same George that I knew, I'll talk your aunt into letting you know her. It's time you had somebody of your own age to play with."

Lalla rushed up the stairs, her eyes shining, and flung her arms round Nana's neck.

"Oh, Nana, if only it was tomorrow afternoon now! Uncle David thinks he was at school with Harriet's father, and if he was he's going to make Aunt Claudia let me know her. Isn't that the most gorgeous thing you ever heard?"

CHAPTER 5

Aunt Claudia

HARRIET'S FATHER *HAD* been at the same school as Uncle David. It did not take Lalla long to find this out, but it took what seemed to Lalla months and months, and was really only three weeks, before Uncle David had managed to see Harriet's father. Meanwhile, Lalla and Harriet met every day at the rink, and every day they became greater friends.

Apart from meeting Lalla, Harriet was beginning to enjoy the rink. Every afternoon just before the session started she collected her skates, put them on and waited for Lalla and Nana to arrive. If there had been no Lalla Harriet would have taken twice as long learning to enjoy skating. Lalla was determined to make Harriet a skater. She could not spare much time from her own practice to give her a lesson, but she took Harriet round with her to get her used to moving on skates, and she saw that Harriet rested only when there was dancing and spent the afternoon moving round by herself.

"I know it's dull just moving along like that, but you've got to do it, Harriet, or you'll never get on to anything more interesting. Your legs look heaps better since you've come skating, honestly they do."

Harriet knew that not only her legs, but all the rest of her looked better since she had come skating. Everybody at home remarked on it, and Doctor Phillipson, when he came to see her, was so pleased that he said he should visit Mr. Matthews an extra time as a thank-offering. The person who was most proud of Harriet's looking so much better was Alec. He felt as though it were he who was making her well, for after all it was his two shillings which paid for the skates, and so when it was wet and cold while he was on his paper round he did not mind as much as he might have done.

"It'd be much worse, the weather being awful," he told Toby, "if Harriet wasn't getting any better. Then I should feel it was all for nothing."

Toby peered at Alec through his spectacles and said:

"Mathematically speaking, if Harriet was not getting well, the fact would be canceled out by the two shillings weekly towards vegetables for the spring."

Alec told Toby to shut up with his mathematical nonsense, but all the same he agreed with him about the two shillings a week. Two shillings a week adds up quickly when it is put in a money box. Besides, to Alec it was more than two shillings a week; it was adventure, the capital that was to start him out on a magnificent career. On scraps of paper in his pockets, in his bedroom and in his desk at school were plans of how he intended his father's shop to look. There were arrows pointing to piles of fruit and vegetables. Each plan covered a different season of the year, and each was so ambitious that had he been able to buy all the things for his plan his father's shop would have looked like an exhibition of fruit and vegetables at a flower show. His vision of what he would buy in the spring was helped by Mr. Pulton, who sometimes said to him when he paid him on Saturdays:

"Twelve shillings for your sister's skates, and two shillings for your dreams."

The way Mr. Pulton said "two shillings for your dreams" dedicated the two shillings for the money box. Although he wanted many things Alec was not tempted to spend anything because, apart from wanting a full money box for himself, he would have felt he had let himself down in Mr. Pulton's eyes if the old man knew he had been buying anything.

What with Harriet's skating and Alec's paper round there was a lot to talk about in the evenings. After the first week's skating Harriet looked so much better that the indignity of going to bed at half-past six with Edward came to an end, and she was allowed to stay up till seven o'clock. Edward was rather annoyed about this.

"I liked Harriet coming to bed the same time as me. I don't think there ever ought to be a minute in anybody's day when they can't be talking to somebody. Now there's me all alone, waiting and waiting for somebody to talk to, and I don't like it."

One night when Harriet had been skating just over three weeks, her father came in from a meeting of the ex-servicemen's association to which he belonged. He told Harriet that he had met Lalla's stepfather there, and what a nice man he seemed to be.

"He hasn't changed much," her father told Harriet. "I remember him perfectly. He told me that Lalla has done nothing but talk about you, and he thought I was going to turn out to be the George Johnson he had been at school with, and that he came to the meeting tonight especially to meet me. He's going to talk to Lalla's aunt about you because he thinks it would be nice, now that you're skating every afternoon, if you could sometimes go to tea with Lalla, and that she might sometimes come here."

After Harriet had gone to bed, and while the boys were out of the room, George told Olivia a few other things.

"He remembered William quite well too. He asked after him and called him by a nickname which I had forgotten—he called him 'Guzzle Johnson.'"

Olivia laughed. "I wish I could tell the children. They would simply love to call him Uncle Guzzle."

George did not answer that, because he was fond of William and would not have had him called "Uncle Guzzle" by anybody. So he went on to say:

"I gather that Lalla Moore's aunt likes the child's nose kept to the grindstone; she's got the makings of a champion skater, and she's not been allowed friends because there's not much time for them."

Olivia thought of the conversation she had had with Nana. "Poor little pet, she had to start skating when she was three. Imagine, she was pushed there in a pram."

"It's difficult, I gather, for David King to interfere. He's only an uncle by marriage, but he's very fond of the child and would like her to have a better time. I rather suspect he's going to suggest to his wife that Harriet would be a good influence for Lalla—skating enthusiast and all that."

Olivia, who had not seen Harriet skating since she started, laughed.

"Poor darling Harriet . . . a skating enthusiast! When she is on the ice she grips Lalla as if she were the only branch to catch hold of before dropping over a cliff."

After Uncle David had seen George he did not waste time. That very evening he told Aunt Claudia about him.

"Met a nice fellow today at a meeting. I was at school with him. Seems his child is a skating friend of Lalla's."

Aunt Claudia was surprised. "Really! I never knew she had any skating friends."

"This child, Harriet Johnson, had been ill and was advised to take up skating for her health. Never been able to talk of anything but skating since."

Aunt Claudia looked thoughtful. A child who had been ordered to take up skating by her doctor, and had become keen in spite of having to skate whether she liked it or not, sounded like an excellent friend for Lalla. Uncle David had not said how long Harriet had been skating, so Aunt Claudia pictured her an experienced skater being trained under a good instructor and entering for tests—though, of course, taking them a long way behind Lalla, and not passing them with the same distinction. Later that evening she said:

"I shall ask Nurse about this child, Harriet Johnson.

A skating friend might be useful to Lalla. She's getting on well and they are naturally proud of her, but sometimes I think she isn't as ambitious as she ought to be. If Nurse says this child is suitable in every way she shall be asked to tea and I will have a look at her."

Uncle David wished Lalla had been there to wink at, but he answered gravely.

"Any child of George Johnson's is sure to be suitable in every way. Nice fellow."

Every day after breakfast Lalla's governess, Miss Goldthorpe, arrived. Alice Goldthorpe had been the sort of girl who was expected to finish up in a blaze of glory as headmistress of a big school. But Alice Goldthorpe had never wanted to be head of anything. What she liked was teaching, and she detested the bother of having teachers under her and being asked to decide things. Because of this she had taught in a great many schools, for sooner or later, in whatever school she taught, somebody had noticed how brilliant she was and tried to make her take a grander position. Each time this happened Alice Goldthorpe had said she was sorry but she would have to leave. Then she had gone to a scholastic agency and asked them to find her a new school in which to teach.

One day two things happened to Alice Goldthorpe: she noticed she was getting fat round the middle (which is called middle-age spread), and an uncle died and left her some money. In his will the uncle said it was enough money to keep the wolf from licking the paint off her front door, but not enough to allow her to fritter away her life doing nothing.

Alice Goldthorpe had laughed when she read the will, because even if the uncle had left her lots of money she would have wanted to do something. All the same she was grateful for a little bit of money, because it meant that she could look round and find the sort of teaching that she would like to do. So she went to the scholastic agency and asked them to find a school which would never want her to take a grander position.

The woman who was head of the agency had grown fond of Miss Goldthorpe and was pleased to see her. She was especially pleased to hear about the money that would stop a wolf from licking the front-door paint. She had jumped up and fetched a letter, and told Miss Goldthorpe that she believed she had exactly the job for her.

The letter was from Aunt Claudia, explaining about Lalla and how she was to be a champion skater, and asking if the agency could find a really good governess to undertake her education. Aunt Claudia wanted a governess who would see that in spite of spending her afternoons on the rink Lalla did as many lessons as other children of her age, and passed the necessary examinations at the right time, and—this was underlined—the governess *must* be someone who, having accepted the position, was prepared to stick to it. Aunt Claudia did not want to entrust her niece's education to someone who was always moving on.

"There," said the head of the agency, "that ought to be perfect for you. This Mrs. King is never going to ask you to take a higher place."

Miss Goldthorpe had frowned at the letter.

"Poor child! What a dreadful life! I don't think I shall like teaching her. I expect she's a horrid little thing, full of self-importance. However, I will go for an interview and find out for myself. There's no harm in an interview."

All this happened when Lalla was seven. From the first moment that Miss Goldthorpe had seen Lalla she had known she would like to teach her, and from the moment Lalla had seen Miss Goldthorpe she knew she would like to be taught by her. More extraordinary still, Nana had approved of Miss Goldthorpe. Nana had been heard to say many times that she could feel in her bones no governess would be satisfactory, that she had never been one for liking governesses in her nurseries, it never worked. Miss Goldthorpe had known in a minute that Nana's bones would tell her things like that, and so she said just the right thing:

"You musn't forget I've always taught in schools. I'm not used to teaching in private houses and am likely to make mistakes. Please help me because I'm sure I'm going to like teaching Lalla."

Nana thought saying "Please help me" showed a nice spirit on the part of Miss Goldthorpe, and though it took time, she came to like her, and in the end to be very fond of her.

The morning after David's talk with Aunt Claudia, Miss Goldthorpe was giving Lalla a history lesson when Aunt Claudia came upstairs. Lalla touched Miss Goldthorpe's arm. She spoke in a whisper.

"I'm sorry to interrupt, Goldie. Listen! There's Aunt Claudia. She never comes up in the morning. What can she want?"

Miss Goldthorpe had heard all about Harriet.

"You don't think Mr. Lindblom has complained that instead of working you're giving Harriet lessons, do you?"

"You know, Goldie dear, it doesn't matter how often I tell you things you always get them wrong. I've told you and told you Max is an absolute angel. He wouldn't think of spying on me and telling Aunt Claudia."

Miss Goldthorpe looked anxiously at the door.

"It's a very unusual time for her to come up, and after all Mr. Lindblom has himself to think of. He's a young man, and you're his star pupil. He's expecting to become famous when you do."

Lalla drew a little skating figure on the edge of her exercise book. It was no good explaining skating to Goldie, she just would not understand. It was perfectly true that she, Lalla, was Max Lindblom' star pupil, and that Aunt Claudia had promised that he should have the entire training of her, but that did not mean he would be so untrustworthy as to complain about her to Aunt Claudia.

"He wouldn't say I hadn't worked—and anyway it wouldn't be true because I have—any more than you'd go to Aunt Claudia telling tales. You know you told her the other day I was well up to the standard for a girl of my age, although you knew that my arithmetic gets worse and worse, instead of better and better."

Miss Goldthorpe looked ashamed.

"I didn't specifically mention arithmetic, dear, and there's plenty of time yet to coach you before you need take your School Certificate. In fact, you might take an alternative subject." Suddenly

Miss Goldthorpe remembered they were supposed to be having a history lesson. "Oh dear, what would your aunt say if she came in? Now, Lalla, I was explaining to you how the Wars of the Roses started."

In Lalla's bedroom Aunt Claudia found Nana. Nina had been tidying one of Lalla's drawers. She heard the door open and, thinking it was the housemaid, did not turn round. It made her jump when she heard Aunt Claudia's voice.

"Good-morning, Nurse. Mr. King met a friend yesterday with whom he was at school, a man called Johnson. I understand he has a daughter called Harriet, whom Lalla meets skating. What kind of child is she?"

Nana wished she knew exactly what Uncle David had said to Aunt Claudia about Harriet's father.

"A very nice child, ma'am."

"Does her nurse bring her?"

Nana knew Aunt Claudia would not approve of children of Harriet's age going to a rink unaccompanied.

"It's her mother I've met, ma'am. A very pleasant lady."

"Is the child a pupil of Mr. Lindblom's?"

Nana swallowed. How awful if she forgot herself and said Harriet was a pupil of Lalla's!

"No, ma'am, she is not having lessons at the moment. She's been ill and it's the exercise she comes for."

Aunt Claudia readjusted her ideas. She very nearly asked if Harriet was a good skater, but luckily for Nana, whose conscience would not have let her tell a lie, she asked instead if Harriet was fond of skating.

Nana beamed.

"She is indeed. Talks of nothing else. Of course Lalla doesn't get much time for talking, what with her lessons and the time she has to do alone on the private rink and all, but Harriet talks to me. Naturally she thinks Lalla wonderful, and she's not the only one."

"Do you think this child's enthusiasm and admiration will make Lalla work harder?"

Nana tried to answer honestly, and luckily she was able to do so. In order to squeeze in time to give Harriet a lesson, and take her once or twice round the rink, Lalla was concentrating very hard indeed on the figures Max Lindblom was teaching her.

"I do, ma'am. You know how it is. A child likes to do well in front of another child, and of course poor little Harriet, all legs as she is after her illness, can't begin to do what Lalla does nor never will."

Aunt Claudia asked if the illness had been catching, and on hearing that it was not, said that if it could be arranged Nana could bring Harriet back to tea after skating on the following Friday, and she would make a point of being in to meet her. Nana said "Yes, ma'am," then opened the door respectfully, and went to the top of the stairs, and waited until Aunt Claudia had reached the ground floor before hurrying to the schoolroom. She knocked. Both Miss Goldthorpe and Lalla thought it was Aunt Claudia knocking, because Nana seldom came in during lesson time. Both their faces showed how pleased they were it was Nana.

"I know I shouldn't interrupt you, Miss Goldthorpe dear, but it's such good news I thought you wouldn't mind." Nana turned to Lalla. "Your aunt says, if it can be arranged, we can ask Harriet back to tea on Friday."

Lalla jumped up. She flung her arms round Nana.

"Giggerty-geggerty, my most beauteous Nana." Then she hugged Miss Goldthorpe. "Angel Goldie, Harriet's coming to tea!

Harriet's coming to tea! The next thing is I'll go to tea with Harriet and meet her brothers. It'll be just like having a family of my own."

On Friday Harriet came to skating in her brown velvet frock. It had been a nice frock, but since she had been ill she had outgrown it. When she heard she was going to tea with Lalla she and Olivia had studied the frock to see if the hem would let down, but they had decided against it. Olivia said she was afraid the letdown place would show badly. Harriet agreed. To make the frock suitable both for skating and for going to tea with Lalla, Olivia made some more-or-less matching pants to go with it. Because of the new pants and because the brown velvet was her best winter frock, Harriet felt quite well dressed when she met Lalla and Nana, but to Nana she did not look well dressed at all. "The poor little thing," she thought, "she really looks better in her old skirt and sweater. Velvet must be good to look right."

Lalla, now that Friday had come, was so pleased she did not notice what Harriet had on; in any case she was not a very clothes-minded child. She had wardrobes full of frocks chosen by Aunt Claudia and put out for her by Nana, but many days, if you had caught her with her eyes shut, she would not have been able to tell you what she was wearing. This was something that Harriet did not know, and when they were on the ice she was a little disappointed that Lalla said nothing about her dress. Instead Lalla warned her about Aunt Claudia.

"You mustn't mind, Harriet, the way she talks. She's my aunt but people can't help what their aunts are like, and for goodness' sake don't laugh if she recites Sir Walter Scott. There's a piece of him she's written under the cups Daddy won, and she recites it at me?" Harriet, busy with her feet, could only make an enquiring grunt, but Lalla interpreted it as a question. "It's to make me ambitious to be the greatest skater in the world."

To Harriet Lalla's skating was too wonderful to be real. The fact that Lalla had special coaching with Max Lindblom, and special practice every day on the private rink as well, made her an important child in the rink world. Harriet was not envious, but since she had been coming to the rink she had thought it must be fun being Lalla Moore.

"How could you be any more ambitious? Anybody would be ambitious being you."

Lalla saw Max Lindblom looking at her.

"I've got to go now." She gave Harriet a push to start her off by herself. "I didn't say I wanted to be ambitious, I said that was why Aunt Claudia would recite."

Max Lindblom took Lalla to the small private rink. He was a tall, fair, rather silent, serious young man who looked upon the business of training Lalla as a very important matter. He himself had thought and dreamed of a skating career ever since he could remember. He found himself puzzled by Lalla, and he did not like to be puzzled by children. He knew all about her father; he had books about him and pictures of him, and thought of Cyril Moore as both a hero and a god.

It had been the happiest day of Max's life when he was given Lalla as a pupil, and as he watched her skating develop, he thought he was a very lucky man. Lalla had a natural gift for skating, and was able to give an immense amount of time to it. Nor was the time spent at the rink all the training she had. There was ballet for grace and balance, and fencing to make her strong and supple.

In his dreams Max Lindblom could see Lalla's name known all over the world, and his name being known too because he had trained her. But sometimes he worried. Why was this little girl with everything—talent, money to spend on it, and first-class training—not getting on as fast as she should? Max hoped he was wrong, but sometimes it seemed to him the reason was that Lalla did not care enough. Then he would laugh at himself. He must be mistaken; the daughter of Cyril Moore must live to skate. He had watched her friendship with Harriet. She had never had a friend on the ice before. He wondered if it was going to be a good thing, for he had to wonder about everything that happened to Lalla. As they walked towards the private rink he asked:

"The little friend is improving?"

Lalla smiled up at Max, glad he had noticed Harriet.

"Yes. I started her going backwards two days ago. She's unsteady still, but that's mostly because she's been ill and she's got legs like a spider."

Max saw how pleased Lalla looked. "She is going to have professional lessons?"

Lalla explained to him how poor the Johnsons were, and how Harriet was only skating to get her legs strong, and how her skating shoes were hired by money earned by Alec on a paper round. She went on:

"Anyway I don't think Harriet would want lessons. She's awfully keen to skate, but that's to get her legs strong and because it's fun."

Max thought perhaps it would be a pity if Harriet stopped coming to the rink when her legs were strong. It would help if she got on so well that she could share Lalla's interest and understand what she was trying to do.

"That is a pity," he said aloud. "She is well built, that little girl, and she has a something . . ." He broke off, not being good at words and finding it hard to explain that the "something" he thought Harriet had was mostly a usefulness to Lalla.

When Harriet came to Lalla's house she thought Lalla's room

too lovely to be true. She even admired the glass case with the skates in it, and the silver cups arid trophies on the shelf.

"I think it's rather nice having things your father won and his skates. My father never won anything much, except a little cup once for golf, but if he had been drowned like yours I think I would like to have the little cup."

Nana looked more approvingly at Harriet than ever. A child who could agree so completely with Aunt Claudia must surely be an admirable friend for Lalla.

There was always a good tea at Lalla's, but because of Harriet there was a special tea with three sorts of sandwiches, chocolate biscuits and a cake covered with pink icing. If there had been such a tea at the Johnsons' everybody would have said how scrumptious it was, but Lalla seemed to take it for granted. She sat down at the table looking at the food with no more interest than if it had been bread and jam.

Harriet had not eaten a great deal since she had been ill, but the tea was so nice that she found herself suddenly hungry. She ate four sandwiches and a piece of pink cake, and was just going to finish up with a chocolate biscuit when the door opened and Aunt Claudia came in. Nana stood up, so Harriet stood up too. She was never expected to stand up at home when visitors arrived, though of course the boys had to, but she did have to stand up for visitors at her school, so she thought perhaps that at Lalla's you behaved as you did in school. It was lucky that she stood up because it pleased Aunt Claudia. She smiled.

"So you're Harriet; I hear you are skating."

Harriet was not usually shy with strangers, but Aunt Claudia was much grander and more glittery than anyone Harriet had ever met before. She hesitated before she answered.

"It's because of my legs. They got wobbly after I was ill, and Doctor Phillipson thought . . ."

Aunt Claudia was not in the least interested in Harriet's legs unless they were useful to Lalla.

"You enjoy skating?" she asked.

"Awfully."

Aunt Claudia studied Harriet. She saw only the top half of her because of the table; the top half seemed to have a great deal of reddish hair and very large eyes in a pale face. She noticed there seemed a neat though shabby brown frock. The child seemed to her to have pretty manners and to speak nicely. She thought that it might be worth while seeing whether she made a suitable friend for Lalla. First, though, Harriet must be made to understand how wonderful it was for her to be allowed to know Lalla, and how important Lalla was. She signaled to Nana and Harriet to sit.

"Go on with your tea." She settled herself in an armchair by the fire. "My brother, Lalla's father, was Cyril Moore, you know. Lalla will have told you how he was drowned. I was his only sister; he made me Lalla's guardian and from the beginning I knew what I must do. I must make my brother live again in Lalla."

Lalla was sitting with her back to Aunt Claudia, with Harriet facing her. Aunt Claudia never took her eyes off Harriet; she wanted to be sure Harriet was taking in what she was told. While her aunt was talking, Lalla behaved very badly. She did not move her body at all, but she moved her face, giving a rude imitation of Aunt Claudia. Lalla's face, as Aunt Claudia said that her father had to live again in her, was so silly that the corners of Harriet's mouth began to twitch, and she had an awful heaving feeling in front as if she must laugh. Nana saw this. She spoke in the kind of voice that would kill any laugh before it started.

"Get on with your tea, Lalla, I want none of your nonsense

messing the food about. And you eat nicely too, Harriet, there's no need to stop eating. Mrs. King wouldn't wish that."

Aunt Claudia had seen the twitch of Harriet's lips, but she knew there was nothing at all about which Harriet could laugh, so she thought the girl was nervous. She nodded at her kindly and said:

"Yes. Go on with your tea. You can eat as well as listen."

Nana put another large slice of pink cake on Harriet's plate. Though Harriet had really meant to have a chocolate biscuit, she ate the cake thankfully, glad of something to do, which meant she need not look at Aunt Claudia. Aunt Claudia went on with her story.

"You must understand that Lalla has never been treated as an ordinary child. All of us who are round her are striving for the same goal, and look upon our lives as dedicated to that goal. First of all, of course, there is Nurse; you have never thought any trouble too great that improved Lalla as a skater, have you, Nurse?"

Nana's face was respectful, but her voice was not quite so respectful as her face.

"Nice manners and ladylike ways and a healthy child, that's what I like to see in my nurseries."

Aunt Claudia was used to Nana.

"Quite, and a strong body and ladylike ways are part of Lalla's training. When she travels all over the world, as she very soon will for international championships, she will not be little Lalla Moore, she will be Lalla Moore, her country's little ambassadress."

Harriet by mistake looked up and saw Lalla making the face of a little ambassadress. She choked over her piece of cake, which luckily gave her an excuse to drink her milk. Aunt Claudia went on:

"Miss Goldthorpe, Lalla's governess, gave up a wonderful scholastic career to take over her teaching. 'Mrs. King,' she said, 'I feel any sacrifice is worth while if I may be allowed the privilege of educating a child with such a future before her.'"

Harriet felt Aunt Claudia expected an answer, so she said very politely: "Yes, Mrs. King."

Aunt Claudia nodded approvingly. "There is Alonso Vittori as well. He has more pupils than he can manage, but when I asked him to teach Lalla ballet he kissed my hand and said that he would be proud. Then there's Monsieur Cordon for fencing—another devotee, isn't he, Lalla?"

Nana saw that Lalla was going to spoil her chances of being allowed to know Harriet by saying the wrong thing, so she answered for her.

"Indeed yes, ma'am."

Aunt Claudia got up. "And now perhaps Lalla is going to have a friend of her own age. But being a friend of Lalla's is rather a special privilege; it means being very ambitious for Lalla and taking as much interest in her success as her teachers. Are you interested in Lalla's success, Harriet?"

Lalla had never mentioned Alonso Vittori, Miss Goldthorpe or Monsieur Cordon. She had spoken vaguely about a governess but there had been nothing to suggest the whole collection of teachers waiting to do nothing else but teach her. Harriet felt as if she were in the pages of a story book. She had never supposed that in real life anybody was treated like Lalla, not even princesses; she could not think of the right sort of answer to make to Aunt Claudia and her face got quite red with trying. Aunt Claudia had made her see a new Lalla, a Lalla traveling all over the world, very grand and very famous, a lucky Lalla who was able to be grand and famous by doing some thing as nice as skating. The thought of this made Harriet's eyes shine. She spoke with real sincerity:

"I think it must be simply gorgeous to be Lalla. I wish I were she."

If Aunt Claudia had been on the right side of the table to do it she would have patted Harriet's head. Admirable child—what a stimulant for Lalla to have a friend who was not only admiring but envious! She nodded approvingly, then looked at the silver cups and trophies. She took a deep breath.

" 'Her square-turn 'd joints and strength of limb, Show'd her no carpet knight so trim, But in close fight a champion grim.' "

Harriet understood what Lalla had said about the reciting but she had no feeling of wanting to laugh. Aunt Claudia made her feel as if she had been out in a very strong wind and had no breath left to do anything. She heard Nana's reverent amen-like "And very nice too, ma'am," and with eyes round with amazement watched Aunt Claudia walk towards the door. It was only when Aunt Claudia's hand was on the door handle that Harriet got her wits back enough to remember the very important thing her mother had told her to say.

"Please, Mrs. King, Mummy says might Nana bring Lalla to play with me on Sunday and stay to tea?"

There was complete silence for a moment, so complete that the clock could be heard ticking, and a piece of coal dropping in the fireplace. Six eyes were fixed on Aunt Claudia. Nana tried not to make hers look pleading, but Lalla's were and so were Harriet's. At last Aunt Claudia nodded.

"I think we may say yes, don't you, Nurse?"

# CHAPTER 6

Sunday Tea

OLIVIA SAID IT was no good making special preparations for Lalla's and Nana's visit on Sunday.

"And don't look so anguished, Harriet darling. You know I always give you the nicest tea I can on Sundays."

Harriet thought her home the loveliest place in the world, and her family the nicest family, but she did think on the Sunday morning before Lalla came that it looked shabby compared to Lalla's home. She knew Lalla would not mind a bit what it looked like, but Nana would and Nana was the one who would count.

The boys had heard so much about Lalla that they had got tired of her. To show how tired they were they mimicked Harriet before she had a chance to say what she had done at the rink. First Alec and then Toby would ask "How's little Lalla today?" or "What did Lalla say today?"

To mark the fact that Lalla, her grand home and her beautiful skating meant nothing to them, both Alec and Toby had meant to be out on Sunday afternoon. This would have been what is known as cutting off your nose to spite your face, for they had a great deal they wanted to do indoors on Sunday, and nothing they wanted to do outdoors. Luckily for them Sunday turned out to be the nastiest, wettest day anybody could imagine, and not even decent rain but a sort of dirty, damp sleet. So when Lalla and Nana arrived they found the whole Johnson family in the sitting room waiting to meet them.

Nana came in first. She took a quick look around. She saw that the furniture was what she called "been good once." She saw that the taste, though not of the sort that she fancied herself, was the kind that Aunt Claudia would approve. Also she saw— and this meant far more to her than the furniture—that the Johnson boys had been brought up nicely, for they all got to their feet the moment she and Lalla came in.

Lalla, almost for the first time in her life, was silent. Coming from her big home, with so much space for everybody and so few people to talk to, Harriet's home seemed gloriously cozy and full of people. Olivia saw what she was thinking.

"Bless you, we surprise you, don't we? You aren't used to a big family, are you?" Then she signaled to the boys to come over. "This is Alec, Lalla."

Harriet did not want Lalla to get muddled about whom she was meeting, so she explained, "He's the one who earns the two shillings for my skates. You know—I told you."

"And this," said Olivia, "is Toby."

Toby blinked at Lalla through his glasses. Lalla thought, though he said "How do you do?" politely, that Toby was looking at her rather as though he wished she was not there. What Toby was really doing was wondering whether he could find out how much Lalla was costing to train, and then work out how much was spent on each cubic inch of her.

"And this," said Olivia, "is Edward."

Edward had been looking forward all day to Lalla's coming; the more people there were in a room the better he liked it. He gazed at Lalla with his enormous, beautiful eyes, and Lalla and Nana, just as Edward knew they would, looked at him with the same pleased faces strangers always wore when they met him.

"I'm so glad that you've come to tea," he said. "I've been hoping and hoping you would."

Nana thought what a pity it was such looks should have been wasted on a boy. They would have been so useful to Harriet, poor little thing.

"That's very nice of you, dear," she said, "and Lalla's been looking forward to coming, haven't you, Lalla?"

Edward beamed at Lalla. "I'm afraid you won't get tea here like the beautiful, beautiful tea you gave Harriet."

Because Edward was so good-looking and so friendly Lalla might have forgotten what Aunt Claudia would say if she asked Edward to tea without permission, but Nana was never carried away by a child's looks. She said briskly she was sure there would be a very nice tea, and in any case food wasn't everything. Edward was disappointed; he had meant to be asked to tea with Lalla.

"Food's a great deal," he said, "especially when it's a cake with pink sugar on it and chocolate biscuits."

"I hope Harriet's told you about Edward," Alec said. "He's a born cad; we do our best, but we can't do much about him."

"I'm not," said Edward. "I like nice things to eat and people being nice to me. It's much duller being someone like you who doesn't tell anyone what he likes."

Olivia laughed and told Edward he was an insufferable child. Then she took Nana and Lalla into her bedroom to take off their things.

At first it seemed as if the afternoon were going to be difficult. It would have been all right if only Lalla had been there, but having Nana to entertain too seemed to make it awkward. But

Olivia soon arranged things so that people of different ages in a small room did not seem to matter at all. She got out some playing cards and suggested that George should play with the children. Then, while Lalla was being taught how to play Casino, she sat down beside Nana and discussed knitting.

Lalla, who was quick, soon picked up Casino and found it the most exciting game. Sometimes she and Miss Goldthorpe played Patience, and sometimes she persuaded Nana to play Snap, but otherwise she had played no card games. Certainly she had never seen a family card game, with everybody trying to do down the rest of the family, and roaring with laughter when they succeeded.

But after tea, when Nana insisted on helping Olivia and George to wash up, was the time Lalla enjoyed best. It was then that the Johnsons sprawled across the table and talked, and told her things which made her feel like part of the family. She heard all about Mr. Pulton and the paper round, and how much money there was in the money box and what it was meant to be spent on. Toby told her that in the spring, when Alec had enough money to start buying things for the shop, he was going to keep a proper profit-and-loss account book for him.

Lalla had never stopped to think where vegetables came from, or what one paid for them, but quite soon she was deep in the discussion of whether it would be better to start spending Alec's capital on early lettuces, or wait for the peas-and-beans and strawberries period. Alec drew for her a plan of the sort of nursery garden he intended to have. And Toby got out an atlas and showed her whereabouts that nursery garden had to be so that the amount of gas used up by a truck bringing in the fruit, vegetables and flowers did not exceed what the fruit, vegetables and flowers would bring in.

"You mustn't mind Toby," Alec said. "He's got a mathematical mind; he can't help it."

Lalla looked respectfully at Toby. "Miss Goldthorpe wishes I had. I can't do sums at all."

Toby thought this was a pity. So expensive an education being given to somebody and she could not do sums.

"What else do you do besides skating?" Alec asked.

Lalla was puzzled. "I do lessons."

Toby saw she had not understood. "Alec didn't mean that, he meant what other things do you like doing? I play chess and collect stamps, and Alec paints pictures, and he's awfully good at games."

Edward felt he was being neglected. "And I sing. I'm going to get a scholarship and sing in a choir school, and I'm the best at acting in the family. I was the prince in the school play, and I'm going to be another prince this Christmas."

Alec rubbed Edard's hair the wrong way. "Not because you can act, you little show-off."

"It's because of his looks," said Toby.

His family looked sorrowfully at Edward.

"We're worried about him," Alec explained. "If he goes on as he is now he's likely to turn out to be a confidence man."

Edward had heard that before. "I needn't. I can't help it if people like me. They talk, and I talk back."

Toby gave Lalla a look as if to say "You see?" Then he remembered that Lalla had not answered their question. "What else do you do but skate?"

Lalla tried to think. There were her books, but she was not what Miss Goldthorpe called "a great reader."

"I listen to the wireless sometimes, and on Sundays, if nobody's in, Nana and I look at television."

Harriet saw that her brothers thought this a very poor answer. She flew to Lalla's defense.

"She goes to Alonso Vittori for ballet, and she fences, and she wouldn't get time for the sort of things we do."

Toby drew a piece of paper towards him. "What time do you get up? How many hours of lessons do you do? How many hours of skating, dancing and all that?" Lalla told him. In the quickest possible time he had the answer. She had two hours of her own every weekday and almost the whole of Sunday. What did she do with those hours?

It was the first time that Lalla had heard anyone suggest that skating by itself was not enough to fill anybody's life. She looked first at one Johnson and then at the other, and saw, to her amazement, that they did not think it was enough. They thought just doing one thing very dull indeed. Ever since she had been pushed in her carriage to the rink, Lalla, at the rink and at home, had been quite a person, and she was not used to having people look at her in a reproachful way; usually their eyes were filled with envy. Suddenly she felt a need to make Harriet's brothers see how important she was. Without knowing it she spoke in rather an Aunt-Claudia voice:

"It's dull doing things alone. I was never allowed a friend before I met Harriet."

It was not only the boys who were surprised, but Harriet too, for Lalla did not sound a bit like herself.

"No friends?" said Alec. "Why?"

Toby did not believe her. "You must have some, everybody does."

Edward beat on the table with his fists to attract attention. "I've simply hundreds and hundreds."

More and more Lalla felt a need to be grand. "My Aunt Claudia didn't know any who were suitable."

"Suitable for what?" asked Toby.

Lalla's face was red; she knew she was being silly but she could not stop. "For me; she thinks a skating champion—I mean somebody who's going to be a skating champion—ought only to have friends who talk about skating."

Toby began reckoning in his head. "How many good skaters are there at your rink? I mean of about your age?" Lalla thought there might be ten, fairly good but not as good as she was.

Toby wrote the figure ten on a piece of paper. Then he put down the number of towns in England. Then he guessed the number of rinks per town. Then he gave each rink ten promising pupils. "It's impossible to get a true figure, but if I were you I'd tell your aunt that your chances of becoming a champion skater are much less than one in a thousand." He could see that Lalla did not know what he was talking about. "I mean if there were a thousand girls in a row, all skating about as well as you do, and about the same age, it's unlikely any one of them would be a champion skater."

Lalla lost her temper. "You're very rude. I'm going to be a world champion. Everybody knows it. You see, my father was."

Toby was about to explain that he wasn't being rude, but that her facts were wrong and he thought she ought to know.

Alec stopped him. "Shut up. If Lalla isn't a champion skater she ought to be, seeing how many people are trying to make her one."

"And you've never seen her skate," said Harriet. "She skates gorgeously, everybody says so."

Alec saw that they had upset Lalla. He thought it was pretty silly to think you were going to be a champion before you were, but he supposed you got like that if you had as many people fawning over you as Lalla had. All the same she was Harriet's friend and their guest, so he tried to change the subject.

"All Toby meant was that it seemed pretty miserable to have nothing else to do except skate. I mean you can't skate at home in the evenings, and we meant what do you do then? Before Harriet was ill she collected things. And she's always making things, aren't you, Harriet?"

Lalla felt that none of them liked her as much as they had, and she was sorry. She did not want to leave with the boys despising her, but the truth was that there was not much she could say; outside skating there was nothing she could think of that she did do. She had a garden, and the boys would have been interested in that, but they would despise the way she looked after it. However, a garden was better than nothing. She mentioned it cautiously. As she had supposed, Alec and Toby were interested at once. They wanted to know how big it was and what she grew in it. Lalla saw it was no good pretending so she told the truth.

"It's a piece of a side border, the end bit. I've got all the proper things for it, a fork, a trowel, a rake and a watercan and wheelbarrow. I used to plant seeds and things; once I made my name in flowers, but Nana stopped helping me. She doesn't like gardening—she hates bending—and she doesn't like getting earth on her hands. It's dull doing a garden alone, so I don't."

"Then what happens to it?" asked Toby.

"It's still mine, but the gardener does it. It really looks like the rest of the garden, but as it's mine I can pick the flowers in it."

Alec thought having a bit of garden was the nicest thing that could happen to anybody. "Do you mean to say you don't plant anything ever?"

Lalla was by now completely honest with them.

"No. You try digging and digging by yourself. It's awfully dull. Besides, neither Miss Goldthorpe nor Nana really care what flowers come up." Then suddenly, looking at Alec, Lalla had an idea. "Alec, why shouldn't you grow things in my garden?"

Slowly, in the way the best ideas behave, Lalla's idea took possession of them all. It was not decided that Sunday afternoon exactly what Alec would grow in Lalla's garden. What was decided was that it should be made use of, and that one Sunday when Aunt Claudia was out Alec and Toby would come round and look at it, and decide what to plant in the spring.

Almost at once a fierce argument went on between Toby and Alec. Alec wanted to try forced lettuces, but Toby, putting down figures and adding them up, tried to make him see that lettuces were out of the question because they had to be grown under glass. An enormous number of them would have to be grown to pay for the glass and, as Toby pointed out, Lalla's garden was only a piece at the end of a border and not a field. He said:

"We'll have to measure the ground before we can tell how the space can be most economically used."

As Toby said that Lalla thought of her garden. What a surprise it was going to be to the gardener when, instead of the magnificent flowers he grew or the candytuft and the nasturtiums that she had grown, he saw tomatoes and cucumbers coming up. He would be so surprised he would be almost certain to talk about it. Lalla warned:

"Don't say anything to Nana yet. She'll have to know, of course. It's better to tell her things slowly. She doesn't like me to do anything unless Aunt Claudia says I may."

Alec had got up and was walking up and down in the room. In his mind Lalla's garden was growing larger and larger, with splendid rows of green peas, and string beans, and even new potatoes. He was brought back from the new potatoes by Harriet's pulling his sleeve. She pulled him down and whispered in his ear. When she had finished he was laughing.

"Harriet thinks that Lalla's garden is a family secret, so we ought to make our pledge over it; and as Lalla's a part of it she ought to make the pledge too."

Harriet danced across to Lalla. "We've always done it; it's to do with our Uncle William. The one who eats the things Daddy would like to sell in the shop." She linked her little finger through Lalla's. "You stand on her other side, Alec, and show her what we do."

Alec linked his little finger through Lalla's.

"It's a family thing but we've always done it. I speak the pledge, and then you say with the others 'Guzzle guzzle guzzle, quack quack quack,' and as you say it we lift our hands above our heads, linked together like this." Lalla felt honored; she had no idea what a pledge was, but she was glad she was being allowed to make it. Alec spoke in a solemn, growly voice. "We Johnsons and Lalla swear on the stomach of our uncle never to divulge what has taken place today." They lifted their hands, and all said solemnly:

"Guzzle guzzle guzzle, quack quack quack."

"That guzzle part," said Alec, as they broke away and came back to the table, "is the most secret family secret. Dad doesn't know that we know that our Uncle William was called 'Guzzle' at school."

"When we found out," Toby explained, "it was the beginning of a secret society—it had to be. That's when we made up the pledge."

"When anything important's going on like your garden," said Harriet, "we make our pledge."

Alec patted his front. "We vow on our uncle's stomach

because it's probably the best filled, and therefore the most important stomach we know."

Harriet looked proudly at Lalla. "And nobody ever, except the Johnsons, made that vow before, so it almost makes you one of the family."

Edward rubbed his cheek against Lalla's sleeve. "I shall like you being one of the family."

Alec gave him a shove. "Shut up, sloppy. As a matter of fact you've a right to share the vow, Lalla, because your garden's going to be a very family thing. It's not only going to pay for Harriet's skates, but it's going to be the foundation of the fortunes of the house of Johnson."

Driving home, Nana thought Lalla looked solemn. "Enjoyed yourself, dearie?"

Lalla wished she could confide in Nana. She would have liked to tell her that the Johnsons were not very impressed by her being a champion skater, that Toby did not think she would be one; but Nana would be shocked, because that was just the kind of thing Aunt Claudia did not want anyone to say. Lalla would have loved also to tell Nana about the garden, but that would have to wait. Nana would not approve of Alec's and Toby's coming to look at it when Aunt Claudia was out. But Lalla could answer about the afternoon.

"It's been simply gorgeous. Oh giggerty-geggerty, it was the nicest Sunday I've ever, ever had."

CHAPTER 7

Inter-Silver Test

THAT SUNDAY AFTERNOON at the Johnsons had a great effect on Lalla's skating. She had often said things like 'Who wants to be a champion anyway?' but she had not meant them; it was like a person's saying "Who's afraid of the big, bad wolf?" when a head-master or mistress sent for him. But hearing Toby say "one chance in a thousand" did something to her. It made her want to hear people like Max Lindblom praise her and say how well she was getting on. And it made her decide to pass her inter-silver test so brilliantly that not only Max Lindblom but everybody else at the rink would compliment her, and then Harriet would go home and tell the Johnsons, and they would laugh at Toby and tell him what an idiot he had been.

With the fine training she had behind her, all Lalla needed to make her excel at the figures that she had to do for the inter-silver examination was to care that she did them well, and to work hard. Quite suddenly she was caring and she was working hard. Max Lindblom, smiling in his shy way, came to Nana.

"Lalla does well. I am very pleased with her. You will tell Mrs. King."

"I will, Mr. Lindblom, and I know she'll be pleased. Very set she is on this skating."

Max was used to Nana, and knew how she felt about skating, and was used to her saying "this skating" in a despising voice; but he knew too she worried if Lalla was not getting on well, and would be glad to tell the aunt that he was pleased.

Nana not only told Aunt Claudia. She also told Wilson, who told the cook, who told the housemaid, and she told Miss Goldthorpe. Miss Goldthorpe, who took Lalla to her fencing and dancing lessons, told Alonso Vittori and Monsieur Cordon, so in the end everybody who had much to do with Lalla knew how well she was doing and smiled at her in a proud way.

A month after Lalla's tenth birthday the inter-silver test took place. The judging was held on the small private rink, and while it was going on skaters who had not been called practiced on the big rink. It had been arranged that Harriet should come to the rink that morning, so that Lalla would have someone to talk to while she was waiting. Lalla did not need someone to talk to, for she was not nervous before a test, but Harriet was quaking at the knees. She looked at Lalla flying round in a new white skirt, sweater and bonnet, and thought how awful it would be if Lalla got her figures wrong, or fell over, or did something else to lose marks so she would not pass.

Because the test was in the morning, and the mornings were her time, Miss Goldthorpe had brought Harriet to the rink. She thought skating rinks nasty, cold, damp places, and she could not imagine why anyone, unless forced like Lalla to do so, wanted to spend her time going round and round on ice when she could spend it reading interesting books. She had not met Harriet until that morning but, as Lalla's friend, she had been wanting to meet her. The first thing that struck her was that Harriet looked worried. "Why," she thought, "should a child of that age look worried?"

"Is anything the matter, dear?" she asked.

Harriet sat down beside Miss Goldthorpe. She put her hands into her coat pockets to keep them warm. "I feel peculiar inside for Lalla. I expect you do too, don't you?"

Miss Goldthorpe had not thought of feeling peculiar for Lalla but she was always interested in new ideas. She thought this one over. "I don't think so. Should I?"

"It's a test. It'd be simply awful if she failed."

"Why?"

Harriet stared at Miss Goldthorpe. Could it be possible that somebody who knew Aunt Claudia could ask why?

"Well, she expects to pass, Mrs. King expects her to pass, and so does Mr. Lindblom."

"How old are you?" Miss Goldthorpe asked.

"I was ten just before Lalla was. Lalla gave me a simply lovely skating book, and Nana knitted me this beautiful sweater, and of course I'd lots of other presents besides."

Miss Goldthorpe said she was glad Harriet had had so nice a birthday, and remembered that Lalla had told her about it. Then she explained that the reason she had asked Harriet's age was to know if she was old enough to have taken any examinations.

Harriet explained that until she had been ill she had been at school, and there had been examinations at the end of each term.

Miss Goldthorpe said that she quite understood, but that it was not end-of-term examinations she was thinking of, but bigger ones. She went on:

"I taught in schools until I taught Lalla, so I was always coaching girls for examinations. Of course it was important that they should pass, but I found it didn't really matter what they knew. Lots of people pass examinations who don't know very much, and lots of people can't pass them who do. Once I got used to this idea I never worried about examinations again. I did my best to make my pupils pass; I couldn't do more. If they didn't, they didn't. I imagine a test's very like a school examination, and that Mr. Lindblom feels about Lalla much as I felt about my pupils."

Harriet hugged one of her knees.

"But Mr. Lindblom doesn't feel like that, nor does Mrs. King, nor does Lalla She's simply got to pass. It'd be the most awful thing that had ever happened if she didn't."

Miss Goldthorpe took a small tin out of her pocket.

"Black-currant drops. They're not at all bad though really they're medicine. You suck one, and don't worry. If Lalla knows her figures she will pass. She's that sort of child. If she doesn't know them she won't, and there's nothing either you or I can do about it. Now tell me about yourself; what lessons have you been doing since you've been ill?"

Miss Goldthorpe was a good teacher because she was really interested in the girls she taught. She thought about them and nothing else. Now, sitting on the side of the rink, she was really interested in Harriet, and Harriet, feeling this, told her everything. About being ill, and the convalescent home, and Uncle William and the shop, and the boys, especially Alec's paper round. It was quite a surprise when Lalla skimmed across the ice and leaned over the barrier and said:

"I've been watching you two. Jabber, jabber, jabber. I knew you wouldn't care about my skating, Goldie, but I thought you'd watch me, Harriet. I've practiced all my test figures, and everyone was watching me except you."

Harriet started guiltily, but Miss Goldthorpe was quite unmoved.

"Harriet and I have been having a nice talk, dear. While she was watching you she was getting quite nervous for you, and I told her it was unnecessary."

Lalla nodded. "So it is, but you can think of me now because I come next."

I'll hold my thumbs, said Harriet. "I always hold my thumbs when anything's happening in the family. It's the best thing you can do to help anybody."

"All right, hold them," said Lalla. "But watch me. I don't want you two gabbling while I'm doing my test."

Harriet and Miss Goldthorpe stood next to Max Lindblom. Harriet was holding her thumbs, but Miss Goldthorpe, who did not believe in thumb-holding, had her hands in her pockets, and so did Max Lindblom. Harriet had never seen a test before, and she had the sort of respectful feeling she had when she went into a church.

Though the two judges looked ordinary, they became, as Harriet watched their faces, taller and more important every minute. They were a man and a woman, and they wore almost identical teddy-bear coats and fur boots. The woman judge had a scarf tied over her head, and the man was wearing a cap. Both carried pencils and cards. Lalla seemed surprisingly at home with them. She searched about the ice for a clean piece where no previous skaters had left a mark, and then stood waiting to begin as calmly, Harriet thought, as if she were waiting to cross the road.

As neither Miss Goldthorpe nor Harriet knew a well-skated figure when they saw one, they could only stare at Lalla and hope for the best. Miss Goldthorpe thought it peculiar to be able to skate, so while she watched Lalla she did not see the child she taught but a new Lalla, whose talent was as weird as the talent of a chimpanzee who could ride a bicycle.

Harriet had been shown by Lalla over and over again what she had to do, and she understood just enough to know which edge Lalla was on, and when she was doing the same figure on a different edge, or backwards instead of forwards. She tried to discover how things were going by glancing at Max Lindbllom's face, but she got nothing from it until Lalla had finished her figures. Then he smiled. When later Lalla's one and a half minutes of free skating were over, Harriet could bear the suspense no longer. She pulled Max Lindblom's sleeve.

"Was she good?"

He was moving towards Lalla but he paused.

"Very good. I am well pleased. I shall ask if we may know her marks."

Lalla, after a charming smile from both the judges, came flying towards Max, her hands outstretched. He held them in both of his, beaming at her.

"That was good, Lalla. You have done well."

In a few minutes, the fact that Lalla had done well was known all over the rink. The top marks she could have been awarded for figures were fifty-four, and the marks she had earned were forty-eight. They were better marks for figures than anybody had hoped for, and extraordinarily good ones for someone who was only just ten. For free skating top marks were twelve, and Lalla had been given nine point three.

Lalla was enchanted with herself. She rushed on to the big rink and let off steam by spread-eagling all the way around it, and in spite of Miss Goldthorpe's waving and beckoning, she would not come off the ice. In fact she would have gone on going round and round if Max Lindblom had not caught her and pushed her to the barrier.

In spite of understanding that Lalla felt wildly excited, and knowing people did feel like that after passing examinations well, Miss Goldthorpe had to make her voice sound severe.

"Come along, dear, it's time we were going home."

When they got to the cloakroom Lalla sat down on a stool next to Harriet, leaned back against the wall and put a foot in Harriet's lap in a lordly way.

"Take my shoe off for me, Harriet. A person who has got forty-eight marks out of fifty-four doesn't feel like taking off her own skates."

Harriet started to unlace the shoe, but Miss Goldthorpe stopped her.

"I'm sorry a person who's got forty-eight marks doesn't feel like taking off her skates, but she's got to for no one else is going to take them off for her."

Lalla felt as though Miss Goldthorpe had tugged her down from the clouds to a common everyday world.

"You are mean, Goldie. Why shouldn't Harriet take them off for me? She's got nothing else to do."

Miss Goldthorpe could see Harriet would be proud to take off Lalla's skates, but she knew that Lalla, who had always had everything that she wanted, could very easily turn into a spoiled little horror, so she answered in a really severe voice.

"Lalla. Take your foot off Harriet's lap at once, and unlace your shoes."

Lalla thought Miss Goldthorpe was being horrible, but she knew there was no arguing when she used that voice. She unlaced her skating shoes and took them off, but while she was doing it she kept up a running commentary under her breath.

"Such a fuss . . . you wouldn't think it would hurt people who've had nothing to do all the morning but watch other people doing things, to take off a shoe . . . it's mean . . . nobody would think here was somebody who'd just got forty-eight marks out of fifty-four."

Miss Goldthorpe said nothing while Lalla was muttering, but when Lalla had changed into her outdoor shoes she buttoned her into her coat and gave her a kiss.

"Shall we celebrate your success? Let's go to a shop and have a bun and something to drink."

In one second Lalla was back in her earlier mood.

"Gorgeous Goldie, you always think of nice things. May Harriet come? And may we have that fizzy lemonade that makes your nose tickle?"

"Of course you may, and of course Harriet's coming. But if Harriet's sensible she will choose hot chocolate, for it was cold by the rink."

They found a very nice shop and Lalla had lemonade, Harriet chocolate and Miss Goldthorpe a cup of coffee, and they all had buns. While they ate and drank Lalla described every moment she had been on the ice taking her test. Neither Miss Goldthorpe nor Harriet understood much of what she was saying, but Miss Goldthorpe managed to look interested, and Harriet really was. Interested faces were all that Lalla needed and she enjoyed herself more and more each minute. When Miss Goldthorpe went to the desk to pay the bill Lalla suddenly remembered another reason why she felt so wildly excited.

"Oh, Harriet, I've thought of something. The very first second you see Toby you've got to tell him about me. How many marks I got, and every single thing you can think of. That'll show him that he's absolutely wrong saying I won't be a champion."

A few days after the test there was more excitement for Lalla. Max Lindblom thought that as she had passed with such flying colors, it would be good for her to have the experience of skating before an audience. He went to see Mr. Matthews. Mr. Matthews was drinking a glass of milk and swallowing tablets for his duodenal ulcer. He listened to what Max Lindblom had to say with a surprised expression.

"But I've been wanting the kid to skate in public for years. We've got that big charity affair in January. Nothing could suit me better. But you've always said you wouldn't allow it."

Max nodded and said, "I do not like a show being made of a small child. A small child does an exhibition badly, but people do not know it is bad, they think it wonderful she can skate at all, so they stamp and scream and applaud. How then can I say to that child, 'you are a naughty one, that was a bad display last night.' The child has heard the applause, and she thumbs her nose at me."

Mr. Matthews looked shocked. "I hope not! I shouldn't like any of our youngsters behaving that way."

"I do not mean they thumb the nose with the hand, I mean they thumb the nose inside the head."

Mr. Matthews did not care what happened inside the head, so he went back to the discussion of Lalla giving a skating exhibition.

"D'you think that aunt of hers would agree?"

Max explained that Aunt Claudia would have liked Lalla to have skated in public long ago, but she had agreed to wait until he said that she was ready for it. He thought now the time had come. He wanted Lalla to learn how a free skating program was made up; that the movements were chosen and the jumps and spins arranged to show her to her best advantage, please the audience, and yet be well inside her range. The only question was who should write to the aunt. Should he do it or should Mr. Matthews? Mr. Matthews said he thought he ought to write. After all, he was arranging the performance for charity and he would say that Max had suggested it.

The result of Mr. Matthews' letter was that one morning Aunt Claudia came up to the schoolroom just as Lalla was starting lessons. It was easy to see, as she opened the door, that nobody had done anything wrong, for she looked like a cat just after it had drunk a large saucer of cream.

"Forgive me for interrupting, Miss Goldthorpe, but I have some exciting news for Lalla. Mr. Matthews asks if you may give an exhibition, dear, at his big charity performance in January. I think we may say yes, don't you?"

Lalla was as surprised as Mr. Matthews had been, for she knew Mr. Matthews had always wanted her to give exhibitions and Max had never allowed it.

"Does Max say I can?" she asked.

"Mr. Matthews says he suggested it. Now when you go skating this afternoon I want you to find out what sort of program he is arranging, because we've got to see that you have a really lovely skating dress for the occasion. I think the first skating frock for our little star ought to be white, don't you, Miss Goldthorpe? With perhaps a sprinkling of silver stars or something pretty like that."

When Aunt Claudia said "our little star," Miss Goldthorpe's insides felt as if they were milk about to curdle. She did not approve of that sort of talk. Time enough, she thought, to call Lalla a star when she was one. However, it was no good talking to Aunt Claudia. So Miss Goldthorpe answered politely, though in rather a stuffy, governessy sort of voice, that she thought white would be very nice indeed.

Aunt Claudia sat down.

"The other thing I want to speak about, Lalla, is your food. Now that you're really on the threshold of success, we must do something about your diet. A skater should be slim, and there are a few naughty curves I should like to see disappear. Don't you agree, Miss Goldthorpe?"

Miss Goldthorpe looked at Lalla's round face, colored like a ripe peach, her mass of shining dark curls, and her nicely made, solid body, and Aunt Claudia or no Aunt Claudia, she had to speak her mind.

"Lalla's not fat. She's nicely covered, and I like to see a child nicely covered."

Aunt Claudia smiled at Miss Goldthorpe in a you-and-I-understand-each-other way.

"An ordinary child, yes. But we can't treat Lalla like an ordinary child. We must treat her like a little race horse."

Lalla was startled. A race horse! She had been wondering what sort of diet she was to have, for the only kind she knew was the sort known as "starve a fever," which happened when she had measles, chicken-pox, and influenza.

"Do you mean I've got to eat oats? I have those in porridge."

Aunt Claudia tried not to look impatient, but she thought Lalla was being slow and her voice showed that she thought that.

"Certainly not oats. We have to increase the proteins and reduce the starchy foods." She turned to Miss Goldthorpe. "There's to be no bread with her luncheon, nor potatoes, and there'll be no rich sweets. I've told Cook it's to be stewed fruit in future. For tea and breakfast there will be rusks instead of bread, and no cakes at present."

Lalla gasped. "Rusks for tea! But I like toast. No cakes!"

Aunt Claudia used her reciting voice. "Not for the moment. We don't mind any sacrifice, do we, to achieve our end?"

Lalla did mind, and she minded Aunt Claudia saying "we." She thought to herself, "I bet she has cakes and toast, and I'm the only one who's got to eat rusks." But she kept these thoughts to herself and merely said:

"I thought I was to have 'square-turn'd joints and strength of limb.' I won't get those eating rusks."

Aunt Claudia gave her a kiss.

"Naughty child. You know I'm only planning this diet because I have to. And believe me, it's not an easy thing to do. With meat rationed as it is, it's going to mean a sacrifice all round to see you have sufficient."

There was a little silence after Aunt Claudia had gone. Miss Goldthorpe was wondering what Nana was going to say when she heard about the diet. Lalla was waiting for Aunt Claudia to be out of hearing. Presently she could be heard shutting Lalla's bedroom door. All the same, Lalla spoke in a whisper.

"She's gone to tell Nana, but I'll get round her. Nana'd never be so mean as to stop me making toast. Do you think I'm too fat, Goldie?"

Miss Goldthorpe struggled to be loyal to her employer.

"Well, dear, I know nothing about skating." Then she broke off and her real feelings got hold of her. "No, I don't, dear. However, if you've got to have a diet, you've got to have a diet, and there's the end to it. Now come on, we've wasted too much time. Where's your atlas? Open it at North America."

In Lalla's bedroom Nana listened to Aunt Claudia's description of Lalla's diet with a respectful face but a turbulent heart. Never had there been a diet in her nurseries except when a child was ill. There had been trouble in the past because a child would not eat, but never when one could.

"Lalla's been brought up to eat what's put in front of her, ma'am, and so she does, bless her. I don't hold with interfering with children's food."

Aunt Claudia tried to be patient.

"But you see Lalla's not an ordinary child. As I've just been saying to Miss Goldthorpe, we've got to treat her with the same care as we would a little race horse."

"Race horse! I don't like to speak against poor dumb animals, but I wouldn't wish it to be said that I would treat a race horse better than one of my children. Same care as a race horse indeed! Lalla couldn't have had better attention since I've had her if she was Princess Anne."

Aunt Claudia wondered, as she had sometimes wondered before, if Nana were getting too troublesome about her work. It would be awkward getting rid of her, for she had been chosen by Lalla's mother and there was some money to come to her if she stayed with the family till Lalla was grown up. The lawyer who looked after Lalla's money was a fairly reasonable man to deal with, but Aunt Claudia had a feeling he might be difficult if she tried to get rid of Nana.

"This is not a discussion, it's an order. But I shall need your help over tea. It would be easier if you would eat rusks too; it's a temptation to the child if she sees a loaf on the table." Aunt Claudia could see by Nana's face that she was never going to agree to eat rusks, so she hurried on. "Now, to a much more exciting subject. Lalla's going to give a skating exhibition in January, so this afternoon I've told her to talk to Max Lindblom about the sort of display it's to be. Perhaps you would talk to him too. I thought her very first special skating dress should be white. What do you think?"

Nana, as usual when she had been interviewed by Aunt Claudia, opened the door for her and saw her down the stairs. Then she came back to Lalla's room and went on with what she had been doing, which was tidying drawers. Suddenly she stopped one of Lalla's socks in her hand. Little race horse! What a way to speak of a child! Rusks indeed! She said aloud: "I've never starved my children yet and I'm not starting now. The moment I see Lalla looking peaky, it's hot dripping toast for her tea and plenty of it."

CHAPTER 8

Christmas

AT CHRISTMAS AUNT Claudia and Uncle David went away to spend Christmas with Uncle David's sister. Always before they had spent Christmas at home, because of Lalla. This year's going away was not something which happened accidentally, as Lalla supposed. It happened because of a talk Uncle David had with Nana.

One day Harriet had brought Lalla an invitation to spend Christmas evening with her and the family.

"We'd have such fun," Harriet told her. "There'll be the Christmas tree, and dressing up, and games, and it'll be twice as nice if you're there."

Lalla looked longingly at Nana. "Nana, do you think Aunt Claudia would let me?"

Nana hated to say no, but she had to. "Not Christmas Day, dear. You have your own tree that evening."

"But there's only me. It'd be much more fun at Harriet's tree."

"That's as may be. But your aunt plans a nice day for you, and would be upset if you asked to go out."

Although Nana had to say no to Lalla at the time, she

thought it a great pity that Lalla could not have a family Christmas for once, so that was why she asked Uncle David to help.

"I don't know if there's anything you can do, sir, but it's lonely for a child, being just the one. It'd be a treat for Lalla, and she's been working very hard, and eating those nasty rusks and all."

Uncle David was fond of Nana, and he could see she was worried. "This diet nonsense isn't disagreeing with her, is it? She looks splendid."

Nana thought it all wrong that a child should look splendid while having a diet, and her voice showed what she thought.

"Not disagreeing at the moment, sir, and I'll soon put a stop to it if it upsets her. I don't want a skeleton in my nursery: No, it's not the diet, it's all work and no play and too much being the only one. It isn't right."

"She has fun at the rink with Harriet, doesn't she?"

"Not really, sir. That poor little Harriet's not a skater like Lalla, nor never will be. She tries hard, and gets on wonderfully, but she doesn't have proper lessons."

"Doesn't she come to tea here sometimes?"

"Just twice she's been, and Lalla the once to her. It's not been easy, what with fittings for Lalla's skating frock and all that."

Uncle David knew what Nana's "and all that" meant. Aunt Claudia had taken to asking Lalla to come to the drawing-room when she had visitors. "This is my little niece," Aunt Claudia would say. "She's becoming quite a skating star. You must take tickets for her performance in January."

Lalla found it a bore being dressed up in a party frock, but she did not mind meeting the visitors. And she got nice things to eat which, now that she was on a diet, she appreciated. She was expected to hand little cakes and canapés around and she usually maneuvered something into her mouth each time her back was to Aunt Claudia.

"You don't approve of her coming to the drawing-room?" Uncle David asked Nana.

Nana looked more worried than ever.

"For most children I'd say yes, sir. It's good for children to be used to meeting people and answering prettily when they're spoken to. But it's not right for Lalla. She's just a bit of the little madam, if you know what I mean, sir, and always was. What she needs is being with a nice family like the Johnsons. The Johnson boys are properly brought up, but they won't stand for any nonsense from a child of Lalla's age. You have to take extra care when there's only one in a family. Three's what I like; three's the size of family a home has a right to expect."

Uncle David patted Nana's arm and told her to stop worrying, and that he would see what he could do. The first thing he did was to arrange that he and Aunt Claudia would be away for Christmas. The next was a splendid idea which was not really his at all. It came accidentally from Miss Goldthorpe.

Miss Goldthorpe had been thinking a lot about Harriet since she had met her at the rink, and so one day when she met Uncle David in the road, and he asked how Lalla was getting on, it was quite natural for her to bring Harriet's name into the conversation. It started with Uncle David's asking if Miss Goldthorpe knew whether Lalla had done anything about Christmas presents for the Johnsons. Miss Goldthorpe explained that Lalla had made grand lists of what she wanted to give them, but so far there had been no shopping because there was not time. She went on:

"I think she's going to trust me to get everything. You see, unless she takes time off from her skating or, special classes, she's never free when the shops are open."

The thought of somebody of ten never being free when the shops were open sounded most depressing to Uncle David. He could not interfere, of course, as Lalla was not his ward, so instead he told Miss Goldthorpe that he would like to help make Lalla's Christmas pleasant and that Miss Goldthorpe could ask him for any extra money Lalla needed for presents. Miss Goldthorpe looked as pleased as if she had had a present. She said:

"That will please Lalla. She wanted so very much to give Harriet some good skating shoes, but of course they'd be too expensive for her. I myself think there are many things Harriet needs more than skates, but Lalla is certain that skates of her own would make Harriet happier than anything else."

Uncle David looked at Miss Goldthorpe's plain, kind face and bulgy figure, and thought what a nice person she was. He said:

"I wish Lalla could see more of Harriet. Nana tells me they don't have much time together on the rink, and of course Lalla's day is so full. It's none of my business, but I'd' like to see her have more fun."

Miss Goldthorpe nodded vigorously.

"So would I. Sometimes when I see her sitting alone at the schoolroom table I wonder if I ought not to try and persuade her aunt to send her to a day school. I should miss her terribly, and of course there are difficulties in the way. Her curriculum does not really allow for a school life, but I feel I should do something. She does spend so much time alone."

Uncle David stared into Miss Goldthorpe's face, and between them the idea was born. Uncle David said it would take some handling, and Miss Goldthorpe said it would be splendid, just what Lalla needed, and she was sure that competition would be good for her work. They both agreed that Nana would be delighted.

"I wonder if the Johnsons would approve," Uncle David said.

Miss Goldthorpe nodded again even more vigorously than before.

"They would. The day I met Harriet she told me all about herself, and it seems that she misses going to school. She was not allowed to go after her illness, because she was not considered strong enough, and now that she is strong enough her doctor won't let her go until the winter's over. He says schools are full of germs and draughts. In Lalla's schoolroom there are no draughts, and between us Nana and I can take care of her."

Uncle David thought for a moment. Then he said:

"Say nothing about this to anyone. You know how I'm placed. I'm only her uncle, but I'll think the matter over, and see if I can persuade Mrs. King. It'd be a wonderful plan."

If Lalla and Harriet had known what Uncle David and Miss Goldthorpe were scheming for them, and what Uncle David was going to try and talk Aunt Claudia into arranging, they would have been even more excited about Christmas than they were. As it was they were mad-doggish. Once it was arranged that Aunt Claudia and Uncle David would be away for Christmas it was decided that Lalla should spend all Christmas Day at the Johnsons' house. She was to go there first thing in the morning, and not to come home till after supper. At teatime both Nana and Miss Goldthorpe were invited for the Christmas tree, games, dressing up for supper.

"And nobody's to mention diet on Christmas Day," said Lalla. "I'm going to eat everything I want to eat—plum pudding and mince pies, and Christmas cake, and as many helpings of everything as I can get in."

There would have been, of course, no chance of a turkey in the Johnsons' house if Lalla had not been going there for

Christmas. Uncle William did not keep turkeys, and if he had he would have eaten them all. But because of Lalla's spending Christmas at Harriet's there came a hamper from Uncle David to George. So that Olivia would not worry about Christmas things, Nana asked Lalla to tell Harriet that a hamper was coming. "And right and proper that it should be, seeing your uncle and Mr. Johnson were such friends at school."

The hamper came two days before Christmas. Olivia saved up opening it till all the family were home. It was an enormous hamper with a big red bow on the top of it, with a sprig of holly through it. Inside was everything Christmassy that was ever heard of. As one thing after another was unpacked and laid on the kitchen table there were gasps and Oohs and Ohs from the family.

Edward rubbed his face against Olivia's sleeve. "Mummy, it's almost Christmas. Couldn't we have one teeny crystalized fruit tonight?"

Olivia explained that the glories of the hamper must wait until Lalla could share them, because her uncle had sent the hamper.

Toby said: "I suppose as Lalla is going to share Christmas with us and her uncle has sent Dad all this, we ought to keep it. But it's unsound policy. We should sell most of this, especially the turkey, which will fetch a lot, and we should eat what Uncle William sends."

The family moaned with horror, but Olivia laughed.

"No, Toby, for one glorious day nothing is going to be eaten out of the shop, except possibly some vegetables—and we wouldn't eat those only I can't be bothered to go out and buy some anywhere else."

Out of doors Christmas Day was dull and gray, but in the Johnsons' house it was so gay it seemed as if the air were glistening. In the morning, almost before the Johnsons had finished breakfast, Lalla arrived, and behind her came the chauffeur with his arms full of presents to go under the Christmas tree.

While Olivia cooked the turkey George took the family to church. It was a nice service with all the proper carols, including "The First Nowell," "Hark! The Herald Angels Sing," and "O Come All Ye Faithful." When they got home again the table in the kitchen dining-room was laid for Christmas lunch. Olivia had made it look lovely, with two red candles, lots of holly, and in the middle something which had come out of Uncle David's hamper: Father Christmas in his sleigh, driving six remarkably prancy-looking reindeer.

The food was so good and there were such lovely things in the crackers, including a lot of indoor fireworks, that Christmas lunch was hardly cleared away and the fat feeling it had brought on had only begun to work off when Miss Goldthorpe and Nana arrived for Christmas tea.

In spite of the splendid cake, nobody could eat much, for not only were they full of Christmas food already but the sooner they stopped eating the sooner they would get to the great moment of the day, presents and the tree.

Lalla had been so happy all day she had not supposed she could have felt happier. Everything was amusing; the family jokes at lunch had seemed to her radiantly funny; helping to wash up and dry, a bore to the Johnsons, was the greatest pleasure to her. But when she was waiting for the Christmas tree to be lighted, she found a new sort of happiness rising in her which gave her a swelling-up feeling inside.

Always before, Christmas Day had been arranged for Lalla, and though she gave presents to everybody in the house, of course, it had been her presents that had mattered, and everybody in the house had stood round to admire and be interested when she opened her parcels. But now she had the thrill of parcel giving. Her insides sort of turned over each time she looked at her special parcels done up in holly-trimmed paper and scarlet bows. "Oh, giggerty-geggerty, won't they all be pleased!"

But Lalla had to wait for the opening of her parcels. Guests first, was Olivia's rule, and she rummaged amongst the parcels, picking out one for Miss Goldthorpe, one for Nana, and one for Lalla. They were all presents from Aunt Claudia. Nana had a grand new work-basket, Miss Goldthorpe an umbrella, and Lalla the latest book on skating.

"Very nice, I'm sure," said Nana.

The first of Lalla's presents to be opened was Alec's. A big book on cultivating vegetables. There was a card inside, which nobody read except Alec, on which was written: "There are six closhes (I can't spell it) as well you know where. Guzzle guzzle guzzle, quack quack quack. LALLA."

Alec was pleased with the book, but when he read what was on the card he gave Lalla a hug, and as he shoved the card into his pocket he whispered, "Quack quack quack."

For Toby there was a new fountain pen to use when he was working out mathematical problems. Edward had a Meccano set that he had been wanting for ages.

But the great present was Harriet's. The shoes and the skates had been packed in boxes wrapped in brown paper, and on top of that Lalla had used her Christmas paper and bows, so it took Harriet some time to unpack. When at last she saw what her present was, her face was so pleased that it stopped looking thin, and seemed swollen with smiling.

"Darling," said Olivia, "I didn't know you wanted skating shoes so badly. Are you getting fond of skating?"

Harriet hugged the skates to her and almost sang. "My own white shoes and skates. Proper white skating shoes!"

Lalla had forgotten what giving the skating shoes to Harriet would mean to Alec, but Toby saw the moment the shoes came out of their box. He said at once:

"You won't give up your paper round, Alec, will you? Imagine, you can save all that money now."

Alec, who was looking at his vegetable book, said "No" and gave Toby a wink. Harriet remembered her manners. She danced across to Lalla.

"Oh, thank you, thank you, Lalla. My own white shoes and such lovely skates! I'll be an absolutely proper skater now."

Miss Goldthorpe put the shoes back in their box. "I believe they'll fit you perfectly, dear. But Sam, who got them for us, said you were to keep them clean and bring them in tomorrow for him to make sure they are the right fit. If not he'll change them."

Harriet hated to see her shoes shut up in their box even for one day, but she knew that skating shoes ought to be properly fitted, and she had a great respect for anything that Sam said. So she let them be put away, though for the rest of the evening she went to the box every now and again and lifted the lid just to be sure they were there.

Mr. Pulton had told Alec to call on him on Boxing Day, which was the day after Christmas. Alec found him in his sitting room wearing his brown velvet coat and cap, and his slippers embroidered in gold and silver thread. He welcomed Alec in his fading, tired voice, but his blue eyes were twinkling and pleased.

"Good morning, young man. This is Boxing Day. Do you know why it's called Boxing Day?" Alec said he did not. Mr. Pulton smiled. "It's the day set aside for the giving of presents or boxes to employees or messengers. I think a boy who carries papers around is a messenger, don't you?"

Alec felt embarrassed. In the Johnson family if you received a present you gave a present. He had not sent Mr. Pulton even a Christmas card, and he had not expected to receive one from Mr. Pulton. It had never crossed his mind that there might be a present. Mr. Pulton seemed able to read what Alec was thinking.

"Boxing Day is a day for giving presents only to those types of persons. A present from an employee or a messenger to the employer would be most unseemly, most."

Alec glanced around the room. It looked very un-Christmassy—not a piece of holly, a decoration or a little bit of paper and string to show where a present had been. He wished he had sent at least a Christmas card. A Christmas card with a horse on it would have been nice; Mr. Pulton would have liked that. Mr. Pulton pointed with his finger to the kitchen.

"If you go through there you'll find some plum cake, and port for myself and ginger-wine for you. Employer and messenger should drink a glass of wine together at this season."

The kitchen was as spotless as when Alec had last seen it. On the table was a tray, on which stood a decanter of port, two glasses, one filled with ginger-wine, and some slices of plum cake. He carried the tray carefully back to the living room, and put it on the table beside Mr. Pulton. Mr. Pulton filled his glass with port, and signaled to Alec to take his ginger-wine. He held the port up to the firelight, so that it glowed like a ruby in his hand.

"Tell me, how is that vegetable garden shaping?"

Alec sipped his ginger-wine. It was good and warming and Mr. Pulton looked interested and encouraging, so in no time Alec was telling him everything, even about Lalla and her piece of garden and the cloches. Then he explained that he would be able to do things now on a far greater scale than he had anticipated because Harriet's Christmas present had been skating shoes.

"You see, sir, that means fourteen shillings a week instead of two for my money box."

Mr. Pulton was a man who respected money; he said: "Fourteen shillings!" in a voice which showed that he appreciated what this meant. "With this fortune do you intend to give up the idea of growing things in your sister's friend's garden?"

"Not really, but she's only got a small bit, I think. We haven't seen it yet, but you can't do much with a small bit. I think in March I shall start spending some of my money on stuff I shall buy at Covent Garden. If we could get a few people used to coming to Dad for decent vegetables regularly it'd be a start. I rather think my first buy will be new potatoes, but Toby's working that out. He's the mathematical one."

Mr. Pulton sat silent for a while, drinking his port and thinking over what Alec had said. Then a coal dropped in the fireplace, and brought him back to the present. He leaned over the arm of his chair and picked up a parcel that was on the floor at his side.

"Here is your box." It was a cash box, a funny, old-fashioned-looking one made of leather, with little iron bars down it, and imitation iron studs all over it. "It's a copy of a very old chest, my boy. Fine craftsmanship, Smell it . . . beautiful leather."

Alec smelt, and found the box had a lovely smell. Then he turned the key and lifted an iron hinge and found how splendidly it was made. Inside there were compartments divided by leather walls.

"I say! Thanks awfully, sir."

"That's all right, young man. When you were here before I spoke to you of horses." Mr. Pulton swept his hand round at the horse pictures in the room. "And you told me about a pony and trap and vegetables, and how some day you wished to be a market gardener. It will be an admirable start if you buy at Covent Garden, but you should not neglect growing things yourself in that piece of garden." He raised his glass. "To your dreams. May you follow them, as I never followed mine."

Because of this talk with Mr. Pulton, Alec told Harriet to ask Lalla if he and Toby could come over and look at her piece of garden before Aunt Claudia came back. Because Aunt Claudia was away and it was Christmas time, it was easy to arrange. The gardener was not coming, or if he came probably he would sit in the kitchen and have tea and Christmas cake. The weather was cold, and Nana never came into the garden in the cold weather. The only person to worry about was Miss Goldthorpe. During the Christmas holidays Miss Goldthorpe came as usual, but only to take Lalla for walks and to her special classes.

One of the surprising things about Miss Goldthorpe was that you never knew in advance what she would think about a thing. When she heard that Alec and Toby were coming over she did not understand why it had to be a secret. She said to Lalla:

"But very nice, dear. It's not really gardening weather, but it'll be healthy for you out of doors. But I wouldn't let Harriet come; she ought not to get her feet wet."

They were sitting by the schoolroom fire roasting chestnuts, which would have shocked Aunt Claudia if she had seen it because chestnuts were fattening. Lalla pushed a chestnut nearer the flames.

"But Goldie, you do see, don't you, that it's got to be a secret? I mean, Aunt Claudia doesn't know that Harriet's got any brothers, and she mustn't know that they come here. Nobody can come here unless she says so, you do know that."

Miss Goldthorpe sighed. She did indeed know. But she had thought that having Harriet's brothers just look at the garden would be an exception.

"I can't believe she'd mind, dear. After all, anybody can be shown round a garden—though I don't think there's much growing at this time of year, is there?"

Lalla took a chestnut off the fire and pinched it to see if it was done.

"You don't understand at all, Goldie. And I can't explain because it's a secret. It's nothing wrong; as a matter of fact it's something good, and it's something nobody but Aunt Claudia would mind. Please, Goldie, would you know where I am if Nana asks, but not know the people I'm with? Nana gets in such a fuss if she thinks I'm doing something Aunt Claudia mightn't like."

Miss Goldthorpe thought of Uncle David's and her own scheme. It would be terrible if it was all muddled up because Harriet's brothers came to the garden and Aunt Claudia found out—though why the child should not be allowed to garden with Harriet's brothers she could not imagine. Still, Aunt Claudia was queer, everybody knew that.

"Very well, dear. But they're not to come without your telling me. When they come you must let me know, and you can slip out to the garden. But I don't like all this secrecy."

The visit to Lalla's garden was a huge success. The piece which belonged to Lalla had been marked out by stones, and though the gardener had taken most of the stones away, there were enough left to see where it used to be.

"The first thing we must do," said Lalla, "is to put the stones back. If we sneak in a little bit of extra garden I shouldn't think anyone except the gardener would notice it—and I expect he would be pleased because it would be less for him to dig."

While Lalla and Alec collected stones to mark out the bed, Toby measured the ground and put figures down in a notebook. He said he thought they might try their luck at early lettuces—anyway the seeds would not cost much.

It was a pity they had not started in the autumn, because a paying thing would have been strawberries. They would not be able to grow much of anything, but then it was not going to cost anything once the plot was planted, so that would not matter.

To her surprise Lalla found that putting stones around the garden with Alec was fun. She had not thought it could be fun grubbing for stones in damp earth, but it was when there was someone to do it with her. So when Alec said that the difficulty was going to be getting the bed looked after, watered and weeded and all that, Lalla found herself offering to help.

"I think Uncle David could get Aunt Claudia to let you come and give me gardening lessons. We could call it that. Aunt Claudia thinks gardening's good for me; it's being out of doors and exercise both at once. But when you can't come I won't mind watering sometimes."

Toby looked at her over his spectacles and said:

"It would be a very good thing if you took up gardening. It's always a mistake to count on just one thing. It'll be all right if you are a skating star"—he put enormous weight on the word "are"—"but if you're not you might be very glad to get a job in Alec's market garden."

Lalla, safe in the knowledge of how well she had passed her inter-silver test, looked at him with scorn.

"It's no good talking like that, Toby my boy. Here's someone who is almost a champion. If you don't believe me you'd better come and see my exhibition. It's two weeks from Wednesday."

CHAPTER 9

Skating Gala

UNCLE DAVID HAD partly suggested to Aunt Claudia his and Miss Goldthorpe's plan for Lalla and Harriet. He knew that with Aunt Claudia it was a good idea to suggest something and then let the suggestion simmer.

This idea took a lot of simmering, for Aunt Claudia could not put her mind seriously on anything until Lalla's exhibition was over. The nearer it got to the gala day the more excited she got. She made all her friends take seats, and found herself looking forward to the night more than she had looked forward to anything for ages. Her friends said, "Dear little Lalla, of course we'll take seats, especially if it's for charity."

Aunt Claudia let them think that Lalla was just a dear little child giving her first skating exhibition; it would be such a moment when the friends saw what Lalla's skating was really like. Already in imagination she could hear the buzz of admiring remarks and congratulations which would shower on her. She listened to Uncle David's idea and brushed it aside. It might be a good plan; she didn't know, she would see what everybody said; if it was thought helpful for Lalla she might consider it. She would not go further than that.

Uncle David had wanted a good moment for George and Olivia to meet Aunt Claudia. He knew it would be a failure if Aunt Claudia met them in their house, because she was the kind of person who expected houses to be large and grand. He thought the skating exhibition would be his opportunity, so he bought three good seats fairly near Aunt Claudia's and sent them to George, with a letter. In the letter he said that he did not imagine this sort of thing was much in George's line, but he would be glad if he and Olivia would bring Harriet, because it would be an opportunity for the two families to meet.

Olivia never bothered very much about clothes; she always managed to look nice, so she took dressing for the skating gala quite casually. But not Harriet. The moment she saw the tickets she fussed.

"Mummy, what shall we wear?"

Olivia was busy at the time and answered vaguely. "Our thick coats, I suppose. It'll be cold, darling."

Harriet saw that her mother had not appreciated the importance of the occasion.

"But, Mummy, it's fur coats arid fur boots. Lalla told me so. She said that Aunt Claudia had said on the telephone to somebody, 'Just a smart warm dress under a fur coat, and of course fur boots.'"

Olivia laughed.

"I've not got a fur coat, darling, and neither have you, and we've not smart warm dresses, and we've not got fur boots. So I'm afraid we'll have to watch Lalla in our ordinary winter coats, with a rug over our knees to keep us warm."

Harriet confided in Nana.

"Mr. King has sent Daddy the poshest seats, and he wants Mummy and Daddy to meet Aunt Claudia, and that would mean me too. Lalla says people wear fur coats and fur boots to things like that, but Mummy and I haven't those."

Nana was as usual knitting. She made soothing, clucking sounds, but her mind was on the problem. It was very important how people looked when they met Aunt Claudia.

"Anything your mother wears is sure to look nice, dear. She's one of the sort who look dressed no matter what they wear." She paused and knitted half a row. While she knitted she thought about Harriet. Harriet's winter coat was in Nana's opinion only fit for the dustbin. And if Harriet took the coat off Nana was sure she would be wearing her brown velvet. If possible, in Nana's view, the velvet was worse than the coat. The coat was just plain and shabby, but the velvet should have been smart. If there was one thing Nana could not abide it was clothes that had once been smart and now were shabby.

"There's a pink spring coat Lalla has grown out of," she said now. "It's nice in the length, but she's a bit square in the shoulders for it. It would fit you nicely, dear."

"But wouldn't Aunt Claudia know it was Lalla's?"

"No. You see, Lalla's got so many things. Besides, although she might notice it at another time, she never would on a night like that. You ask your mother if you can borrow it, and if she says yes I'll bring it along and an extra warm sweater of Lalla's to wear with it. The ice strikes up very cold, and you don't want to catch a chill."

The night of the skating gala every seat at the rink was taken. It was an annual event in aid of local charities, and was always a big occasion. All types of skating celebrities gave exhibitions: professionals, championship soloists and pairs, champion figure skaters and champion dancing pairs. There was usually an exhibition by promising local children as well. Sometimes it was a skating ballet arranged for a lot of children, sometimes it was a pair of children ice dancers, and now and again it was a solo exhibition.

Lalla, as her father's daughter and an unusually promising child, was given a star place on the bill. She was to come last in the first half before the intermission.

Nothing that could contribute to Aunt Claudia's approval of the evening had been forgotten. Mr. Matthews met her in the entrance and gave her a beautiful bow, and told her how proud she was going to be of Lalla in a loud enough voice for all the people coming in to hear. He himself took her and Uncle David to their seats, which were the best place at the rink, and stayed a few moments saying polite things.

When Mr. Matthews had gone Aunt Claudia looked round and found her friends were trying to attract her attention by waving their programs. One of the things that pleased her most about the evening was that Uncle David had not only agreed to come but came willingly. This had been a great surprise. She thought how good looking he was, and guessed how envious everyone must be of her; such a handsome husband and a niece who was the star child of the evening. She did not know that Uncle David's being there was part of a scheme and that while she was waving to her friends, he was waving to George and Olivia.

"Is that your friend David King?" Olivia asked.

George nodded. "Not a friend really, you know. Surprised he remembered me."

Harriet, feeling very grand in Lalla's nice-fitting pink coat and snug in her pink sweater, pulled at her mother's arm and said:

"The lady beside him is Lalla's Aunt Claudia."

Olivia was going to say that nobody could suppose the grand lady in mink was anybody but Lalla's Aunt Claudia, when she looked at Harriet. Pink was not her color, poor pet; it did not go with reddish hair and rather a pale face. Harriet was getting on splendidly, but she still had too much eyes for the rest of her. She was so proud in her pink coat, and so in awe of Aunt Claudia, whom presently they had to meet, that Olivia knew it was not the moment to speak jokingly.

"Isn't she grand, but no grander than you look, darling. I shall feel as though I ought to curtsy when you two are speaking to each other."

The performers in the gala waited for their entrances on the small rink, so that they could warm and limber up before they went on. Nana had a seat reserved at the end of the rink next to Miss Goldthorpe, but she was not going to use it until Lalla went on. In the meantime she sat and watched her, holding Lalla's white ermine coat on her knee.

Nana did not really hold with what she called "making a show" of Lalla. Little private theatricals were nice for a shy child, but Lalla was not shy and did not need bringing forward. Moreover, she was being kept up past her bedtime for no purpose, so Nana was rather disapproving. But as she watched Lalla practicing, the disapproving feeling wore off and she felt proud.

Lalla was wearing a white ballet dress with a bodice of white satin, and net and tarlatan skirts which glittered with silver stars. On her head, in place of the bonnets she usually wore, was a small cap of *diamanté,* which held her curls in place.

Nana saw that the grown-up skaters watched Lalla with pleased faces, thinking how sweet she looked, which she did, the pretty lamb. Nana still disapproved of dieting her, but had to admit that Lalla did not seem any the worse for it. And in her ballet dress, with that tight satin bodice, it was a good thing she didn't stick out in front as she had done a week or two back. Aunt

Claudia had succeeded in buying a pair of the most beautiful nylon tights. When Nana had first seen them she had been most sniffy about them.

"Nylon tights! Lot of foolishness; catch her death. She should be wearing her white wool same as usual."

Lalla had giggled.

"Silly Nana! I couldn't have worn wool anyway. With a ballet dress, it would have to have been bare legs. Nobody could wear wool tights with a ballet dress."

Now that Lalla had the tights on Nana saw that she was lucky to have them. Many of the skaters had bare legs, and very cold Nana thought it looked, giving a hasty bluish tinge to the skin. If a child had to do a foolish thing like stripping to go on the ice in midwinter, then it was better to wear nylon than nothing at all. One thing she had seen to—and it comforted her to know that she had seen to it—Lalla was wearing good wool next to the skin, wool knitted by Nana herself.

Max Lindblom had arranged a program for Lalla to fit into a specially orchestrated mixture of music from "Where the Rainbow Ends." A few bars were played before her entrance, and then, as she skimmed onto the ice, she was picked out by a frosted spotlight. The fairy music and Lalla's fairylike appearance, and the magic quality of the cold, blue light on the ice, was enchanting; her entrance got a spontaneous burst of applause.

Lalla had not felt nervous before she came on; she enjoyed free skating and was happy performing the routine Max had arranged for her. It included most of the jumps she liked best and spread-eagling as well, which she adored. She was enchanted at receiving a round of applause, smiled gaily and settled down to enjoy herself.

The program Max had chosen was not difficult, and no

knowledgeable person would have been fooled into thinking that it was. What was noticeable about Lalla was her gaiety. That she was finding every minute of her exhibition fun bubbled out of her and made the audience think it was fun too. When, at the end, she skimmed down the rink in an arabesque, her arms outstretched, and curtsied to the best seats—which really meant curtsying to Aunt Claudia—the audience not only clapped but cheered.

Lalla had to take six calls, and on the sixth Mr. Matthews, very nervous because he was not wearing skates and was afraid of falling down, came on the ice and presented Lalla with an enormous bouquet of pink carnations.

Olivia turned to Harriet, her eyes bright and her cheeks very pink with pleasure.

"Darling! How lovely Lalla is! The pet can skate, can't she?"

Harriet glowed. Being Lalla's friend was almost as grand as being Lalla. She said proudly:

"And she can do much more glorious things than that, terribly difficult things that lots of people who've learned skating for years and years can't do."

George lit a cigarette. He was watching Uncle David with Aunt Claudia. He turned to Olivia and said:

"I doubt whether King will be able to make that introduction. Look at the aunt." They all looked.

Aunt Claudia was in a dream-come-true world. She had always known that Lalla could skate, always known that she would be a star, but this was the first time she had felt what it was like to own Lalla. Years ago she had found it made her important to be Cyril Moore's sister, and she had liked the feeling, and had missed it when he was drowned. But being Cyril Moore's sister was a mere nothing to being Lalla's aunt and guardian. Everybody she knew and lots of people she did not flocked round her saying the nicest things, and the nicer the things they said the grander Aunt Claudia felt.

It was only just as the intermission ended that Uncle David managed to introduce the Johnsons. By this time a smile had become part of Aunt Claudia's face, and a rich graciousness so much a part of her voice that it was almost as if she were talking with a piece of cream out of a chocolate bar lying on her tongue.

"This is my friend George Johnson, Harriet's father," Uncle David explained, "and this is Mrs. Johnson, Harriet's mother. How do you do, Harriet? You and I haven't met before, but I've heard a lot about you."

Aunt Claudia was too carried away by the glory of the evening to see anybody as clearly as usual, but not so carried away but that some part of her mind said to her that Olivia, though obviously poor, was charming in every way, that David's school friend George seemed presentable, and that Harriet looked better dressed than when she had last seen her. Because she was feeling pleased with everyone and everything, Aunt Claudia was in the mood to say nice things, and as she looked at the Johnsons the suggestion made by Uncle David at Christmas came back to her. She smiled kindly at Harriet.

"I hear this child has not been going to school since her illness. It might be possible for her to have lessons with Lalla. Of course nothing can be arranged in a hurry. Naturally everything planned for Lalla has to have great thought. But perhaps I might give you a ring sometime, and you would come to tea and discuss it."

The idea of Harriet's doing lessons with Lalla was so new to the Johnsons that they stared at Aunt Claudia in silence. Then Olivia rose as usual to the occasion. She said:

"What a lovely idea! But of course it would want think-ing over."

As soon as she was back in her seat, Harriet put her hand into her mother's. "Mummy! Do you think she meant it? Lessons with Lalla and Goldie every day? Wouldn't that be simply gorgeous!"

Lalla's success at the skating gala made Lalla less nice to have as a friend than she had been. Lalla had what is called a vivid personality, which was the part of her that made her remembered and stand out from other skaters. Because she had this, the sports writers noticed her and wrote about her in their papers, and photographers took photographs of her.

If Nana and Miss Goldthorpe could have had their way, Lalla would never have read about herself in the papers, or looked at the photographs. Aunt Claudia, however, thought that it would stimulate Lalla to further efforts. Many days she had her down to the drawing room after tea and read the press notices out loud to her.

"Little Lalla Moore, Cyril Moore's daughter, is a skater of re-markable promise, of whom we should hear more." "Little Lalla Moore, the daughter of figure skater Cyril Moore, was the star of the evening." "Little Miss Lalla Moore, for whom a great future is predicted, won all hearts." And in the Sunday papers, under pic-tures, "A Young Skating Star." "A Winsome Child Skater." "A Pretty Little Queen of the Ice."

The more press cuttings Aunt Claudia read or showed to Lalla the more prancy and difficult to deal with Nana and Miss Goldthorpe found her. It was difficult to get her back from what Nana called being above herself. Aunt Claudia wanted her to be above herself. Wilson, the cook, and Helen, the housemaid, did not mind her being above herself. They cut out photographs of her, and stuck them up in their bedrooms, in their sitting room, and on the kitchen mantelpiece, and liked it when she came in and told them all about the gala.

Harriet tried not to side with Nana and Miss Goldthorpe against Lalla, but she did wish her friend would stop being grand. Lalla had always been inclined to order Harriet to do things for her, and after the gala she treated Harriet rather as though the girl existed for no other purpose than to wait on her.

"Don't you give in to her, dear," Nana told Harriet. "The way she goes on you'd think you were no more than a heathen slave that she'd bought. You want to say no to her sharp and plain, same as I do."

Miss Goldthorpe said: "I do hope Mrs. King will soon come to a decision about your doing lessons with Lalla, Harriet dear. It's going to be so good for Lalla to have someone to work with, and you must not give in to her. She needs a friend who doesn't give in."

Nana and Miss Goldthorpe's great supporter in putting Lalla back to being an ordinary girl who skated rather nicely was Max Lindblom. He spoke to Nana most seriously about his star pupil.

"It is not good that Lalla is shown these press cuttings. She thinks now she is so clever she need not work. But I tell you that she must work harder than ever if she is to pass the test for her silver medal in May. I cannot make her concentrate on her brackets."

To Nana a bracket was something hung on a wall, on which ornaments stood, but she was accustomed to hearing Lalla and Max using words which meant nothing to her.

"I'll speak to her about it, Mr. Lindblom. She's been a bit of a madam lately, but it should be passing off soon. Children are apt to get above themselves occasionally, but I'll tell her plainly that you're not pleased, and she's to think of those brackets, or we'll have to be bracketing her."

Lalla was not the only member of the household to get above herself after the skating gala. Aunt Claudia was above herself too. Often she thought about that night, about the way the manager at the rink had received her, the applause, and the admiration and envy of her friends. She remembered watching the rest of the entertainment with Lalla's bouquet on her knee, and people whispering about her, pointing her out and saying who she was; and she remembered leaving the rink and strangers coming up and saying nice things. It was a new sort of world to her, and she wanted the same excitement to happen again very soon.

Aunt Claudia went to Mr. Matthews, who ushered her into his office and sat her in his best armchair. He told her how pleased he was to see her, and how proud he was of the success Lalla had made at his gala. Aunt Claudia leaned forward.

"It's about that I've come to see you. I think an experience like that is good for Lalla. You won't believe it, but there have been times when I've felt, not exactly a lack of enthusiasm on her part, but a lack of ambition. Now I see why. The child needed a taste of success and applause."

Mr. Matthews looked at Aunt Claudia politely, but inside he was surprised. He was used to skating mothers pushing forward their own little darlings, and making a fuss if another child was given a chance that their child did not have, but he had not placed Lalla's aunt as the type. He had looked upon her as a strict guardian who saw in Lalla a child who might follow in her father's footsteps and become a fine skater, and who was prepared to spend a great deal of money to achieve this.

An Aunt Claudia who wanted Lalla made a show of by

giving public performances was a new idea to Mr. Matthews, but he was a businessman and quickly saw two things. One, that it would bring credit on his rink if Lalla were allowed occasionally to appear for charity, and the other that Max Lindblom must not be told what was planned. Mr. Matthews picked up any gossip that was around his rink as if he were a vacuum cleaner picking up dust. That Max thought Lalla's success had gone to her head was gossip that had blown in from every quarter. Mr. Matthews drew a diary towards him.

"There will not be many important events before the season ends, but there are two at which I should be glad if you would allow Lalla to perform. One is in London, and one out of town. Of course you will have no trouble with the arrangements. The hotel bookings for the out-of-town date will be made by the management of the rink concerned."

Aunt Claudia had a vision of herself, Lalla, and Nana walking into a large, expensive hotel, and of herself being pointed out as "Mrs. King with her niece, the little skating star." She saw herself returning in the evening, carrying Lalla's flowers, and allowing her fellow guests to crowd round her and congratulate her. She told Mr. Matthews that she thought they could manage the two dates, and that she would see about Lalla's frocks right away.

"I must plan quite a skating wardrobe for her before the winter season starts."

Mr. Matthews put his finer tips together and asked cautiously if Mrs. King had discussed these additional public appearances with Max Lindblom.

Aunt Claudia felt Mr. Matthews was not asking from idle curiosity, so she said "no," and asked why.

Mr. Matthews pressed his fingers more tightly together than ever, and hoped he was being tactful when he said:

"Skating instructors are apt to think that only work on the figures for the tests is advisable before a test. With her silver test coming in May, I think you may find Max Lindblom difficult to deal with."

Aunt Claudia, having decided that public appearances were good for Lalla and knowing they were good for herself, was not prepared to let Max Lindblom spoil things. She gave the sort of laugh that means "Who cares?" and said:

"Then I shan't tell him; I think I know what's good for Lalla, and I'm sure you do."

After Aunt Claudia had gone Mr. Matthews telephoned about Lalla to the managers of the two rinks which were having charity performances. After that he sat down, meaning to get on with some other work, but the thought of his talk with Aunt Claudia kept interrupting him, and quite suddenly he said something out loud which surprised him very much, because it was "poor little kid."

When Max Lindblom heard that Lalla was going down to the south coast to skate at a charity gala he was very angry indeed. It happened to be a day when Miss Goldthorpe was at the rink, so she heard all that Max thought about it.

Except when she was talking to Harriet, Miss Goldthorpe filled up her time at the rink with her favorite occupation, reciting Shakespeare in her head. She was a great lover of Shakespeare's plays, and could recite them for hours on end and never repeat herself once. That particular day she was with Henry V. She was saying to herself "O for a Muse of fire" and imagining the rink had turned into "this wooden O" and that she was breathing the casque-filled air that did affright at Agincourt, when Max sat down beside her and spoke rapidly in her ear.

Miss Goldthorpe took her time coming back from Agincourt and missed the first part of what Max was saying. When she could give him her attention she found that on the subject of Lalla he and she had ideas in common.

"That one exhibition, yes," Max was saying. "I had thought it was good for Lalla. I myself suggested it. But it was not good. Now she is the great star, she knows everything. 'Do not bother me, Max, I'll do those silly old brackets in plenty of time for my test.' But I tell you," and here Max thumped his chest, "that she will *not* do them unless she works and works. There is no time for her to go away skating, and if she does she'll be even more diffi-cult to train. Applause goes to her head like the glass of wine. This must not be."

Miss Goldthorpe looked at Max, and thought what a pity it was that such fire and earnestness should be wasted on so poor a cause as skating.

"I'm sure you are right, Mr. Lindblom, but you are wasting your energy being angry with me. I have nothing whatsoever to do with Lalla's skating. I educate her."

Max became even more frenzied. "Then you know how I feel. You must go to this aunt, and you must say Lalla may not perform in skating galas because it interrupts her education."

Miss Goldthorpe looked again at Max. What a pity that such agile legs should not be allied to an equally agile brain. Clearly this young man's brain was not only not agile but scarcely a brain at all. Else why, having met Aunt Claudia, should he suppose that she or anybody else could tell Aunt Claudia what Lalla might or might not do? Such volubility wasted on such mistaken thinking made Miss Goldthorpe sad. She patted Max's knee and said:

"Keep calm. Now think. You know Mrs. King will not be told what is best for Lalla. She is the only one who knows. If you or I or anybody else tried to argue with her all that would happen would be that we should cease to teach Lalla."

Max put his head in his hands. "Then all is finished."

Miss Goldthorpe felt sorry for him, for he seemed to her pathetic and no older than Lalla. She spoke bristly as she would to a child who was upset.

"Nonsense. Now take your head out of your hands and listen to me. You can't prevent Mrs. King from allowing Lalla to skate at charity performances, but you *can* do something to help Lalla. Her old nurse says that Lalla has got above herself, and that describes it exactly. Now the remedy I suggest is the company of another child Mrs. King is already half wedded to the idea of Harriet spending the day with Lalla and doing lessons with her. If you, quite on your own, would suggest that Harriet would be a help to Lalla's career, I think the affair could be settled. There's nothing so good for a spoiled child as the company of another child of her own age."

Max raised his head and looked at the rink. Lalla was watching Harriet struggling with what Max's eye recognized as forward outside threes, and what Miss Goldthorpe supposed was the sort of playing about which would end by Harriet's falling on the ice. As Max watched the two children he began to look less distraught. Then, after a bit, his face assumed the sort of cheerful look people wear when they are thinking about something they like to think about.

"I shall see Mrs. King. I will tell her that I think it is good for Lalla that her friend Harriet should take lessons and be on the small private rink when Lalla practises her figures. I have watched the little friend. She wastes no time; she is absorbed, that one. She will not be able to know how a bracket should be, but she can watch Lalla and be interested, and then perhaps Lalla will work."

Miss Goldthorpe was glad that Max could grasp so quickly what she had in mind, and began to think better of his brain. When he got up to go she asked when he intended seeing Mrs. King, and was delighted find that he not only moved fast on his legs, but evidently moved fast in things that he did.

"I go to Mr. Matthews now. By tomorrow it will be arranged."

Not "by tomorrow," but by the day after, it was arranged. Mr. Matthews telephoned Aunt Claudia and asked if she would see Max Lindblom, explaining what it was about. That same evening Uncle David telephoned George and asked if Olivia could come to tea the next day to discuss the whole thing. Finally Aunt Claudia told Lalla and Nana, and Olivia told Harriet.

Harriet was breathless with pleasure. "All day! Tea too?"

Olivia kissed her. "Lalla's aunt wanted you to go to tea every day, but I wasn't having that. We should never see you at all, darling. Sometimes, of course, you can go back with her, but often, I hope, you'll bring Lalla and Nana to tea here."

Lalla asked the same question.

"And tea, and after tea a bit?"

Aunt Claudia looked annoyed.

"That's the one tiresome thing. I invited Harriet to come back to tea every day, but her mother said that would mean they wouldn't see enough of her. I've had to agree that now and again you may go to tea there as a change."

The night when everything was decided, Lalla and Harriet danced their way to bed.

"Mummy," said Harriet hugging Olivia, "you do know I'll

miss being with you all day, but skating lessons! It's probably the most gorgeous thing that that'll ever happen to me."

Olivia put her arms round her.

"Is it, my pet? You are a funny little scrap. Who would have thought that less than six months ago you'd never seen a skate?"

Lalla butted Nana, who was trying to tuck her up, with her head.

"You wait and see my 'square-turn'd joints, and strength of limb' after I've had Harriet almost to live with me. They'll grow so square-turn'd and so strong they couldn't be squarer or stronger."

Nana kissed Lalla good night.

"Lie down, and let's have no more foolishness. You don't want to get any squarer than you are or there'll be more of that dieting."

CHAPTER 10

Silver Test

LESSONS FOR BOTH Lalla and Harriet became fun, and Miss Goldthorpe enjoyed them enormously. The two girls were not only almost exactly the same age, but much of a muchness at lessons. Lalla was good at things like grammar and remembering dates and geography, and Harriet loved reading. Both girls were bad at, and detested, sums. But it was fun being bad at the same thing. Lalla found even adding money, which she thought the nastiest kind of sums, could be pleasant if it meant she beat Harriet when she got the total right. She did not share Harriet's and Miss Goldthorpe's taste for literature, especially not their fondness for Shakespeare's plays.

"I wouldn't have thought it of you, Harriet," Lalla would say. "You don't look the mimsy-pimsy sort of person who could like hearing about that silly Viola and that awful Malvolio."

At eleven the door would open and Nana would come in with glasses of milk for the girls and a cup of tea for Miss Goldthorpe and biscuits for everybody. Sometimes she would bring her own cup as well; and while she drank her tea would give a running commentary on how things were going in the house.

"Your aunt's out for a fitting for her clothes for that Ascot. Cook has a chip on her shoulder this morning. She meant to go out with her sister this evening to the pictures, but now Wilson's brought a message from your aunt to say there'll be two extra for dinner. The sun's coming out beautifully, and the gardener says you ought to come down and see his crocuses; proper sight they are on the lawn."

When Nana mentioned the gardener Lalla and Harriet would exchange looks with Miss Goldthorpe. It was time the boys came over and dug up that bed and put in their lettuce seed. According to Alec it should have been planted some time before, and the little plants growing under cloches.

Usually Nana would finish with a bit of news for Harriet. She would say she had been going through Lalla's drawers and cupboards and had found this thing or that thing which would be useful to her. The things she found were always worn in the house; they never went back to Harriet's house. Nana had not talked to Miss Goldthorpe about Harriet's clothes. It was no good talking to Miss Goldthorpe about clothes; she never knew what anyone had on, or cared what she looked like herself, but now and again Nana had confided in her about the Johnsons.

"They haven't any money, poor things, and Mrs. Johnson so nice and all. I don't want her knowing, but never being sure when Mrs. King will pop in and out of the schoolroom, and knowing how she expects the children to look, I find the easiest thing is to use Lalla's clothes for both. As soon as Harriet comes I say 'Take that off, dear, we don't want it spoiled,' and I've popped her into something of Lalla's before you can say Jack Robinson."

Usually Nana's news for Harriet would come just as she was picking up the tray.

"After your dinner, Harriet, I'd like to see you in Lalla's room. I've an old frock of hers, more than good enough for lessons. It will fit you nicely if I take it in and let it down."

At twelve o'clock on Mondays and Thursdays Miss Goldthorpe walked the children around to Alonso Vittori's studio for Lalla's dancing class. Alonso Vittori was a leading stage dancer, but he took a few private pupils as well. He had been teaching Lalla for some time. He did not have to give her a strict ballet training, but more a good grounding, so that she learned to hold postures and move her body and hands gracefully. Of course ballet exercises were very good for her legs also. Alonso was fond of Lalla as a person, but not really fond of teaching her dancing, because Lalla thought learning dancing a waste of time. "Not that beastly exercise again, Alonso darling. Why should I have to do it, I'm a skater? On my skates I couldn't do that, so why should I learn it on a floor?"

To begin with, after Harriet had joined Lalla for lessons, she had watched her being taught to dance with the same open-eyed admiration as when she watched her skating. How extraordinary for legs to do that! How clever of Lalla to have legs that did that!

At the end of the third lesson, at which Lalla had been particularly tiresome about barre exercises, Alonso noticed Harriet's admiring face. Other people might think Harriet too big in the eyes, and too thin in the legs, but Alonso admired her; he liked her thin look, and thought it a pity that now Lalla had Harriet to work with she should be a devoted admirer instead of an ordinary critical friend. So he went across to her.

"Why don't you join the class next time?"

Harriet blinked at him in astonishment.

"Me! But I couldn't."

Alonso told her not to be silly.

"Take off your hat and coat, put on Lalla's shoes, and go over there."

Harriet felt rather shy standing all alone in the middle of the room in ordinary school clothes, trying to do what Alonso told her while Lalla and Miss Goldthorpe looked on, but Alonso did not think too badly of her. Just before he finished with her he called Lalla over.

"Have a look at that. Harriet's never learned, but she's holding her hands better than I've ever succeeded in making you hold yours."

It was not absolutely true, but it was near enough true for Alonso to think he might say it, and it certainly had the desired effect on Lalla. She had never been jealous before but she had never had cause to be. She gave Harriet a push, and told her to take off her shoes, and told Alonso he was only saying that to annoy her. Alonso laughed, rumpled Lalla's hair, and told her that from now on Harriet was to attend his classes, and he expected she would have to work hard to keep up with Lalla.

Lalla had never needed to be told to work hard at fencing. She liked it, and found it fun, but Monsieur Cordon had often thought it would be good for Lalla to have a child of her own size to fence with. He ran his fencing classes with the aid of his sons, and as they had a great many pupils, it was not always convenient for him to fence with Lalla or to spare one of his sons to give Lalla full attention for half an hour. So when he discovered that Harriet was always coming to watch his classes, he decided she should learn to fence too, and he told one of his sons to instruct her.

Monsieur Cordon explained what he was doing to Miss Goldthorpe. "It is nice that Lalla should have her little friend fencing too. Fencing for Lalla is for the good of her figure, and for quick movement. She will never wish to study it seriously. If her friend fences that will be admirable for all."

Miss Goldthorpe recited Shakespeare to herself through both ballet and fencing classes. Usually the clash of the foils took her mind to the more fiery scenes. On that day she was present in imagination at the duel between Hamlet and Laertes. She was hearing the king say: "Let all the battlements their ordnance fire" when Monsieur Cordon spoke. She liked Monsieur Cordon, as she liked the other odd people who instructed Lalla. To her it was past comprehension why an apparently pleasant Frenchman and his two pleasant sons should waste their time playing about with foils, when dueling had gone out of fashion years ago, but she tried never to let him know that she thought he was frittering away his life. She only caught half of what he said, but it was enough for her to understand that he was suggesting teaching Harriet. She began to wonder if she could be misjudging Lalla's teachers; they were all showing more sense than she had anticipated. She smiled at Monsieur Cordon and thanked him, and said nothing could be better for Harriet, whose legs needed strengthening because she had been ill.

On Wednesdays and Saturdays, when there were no special classes, Lalla and Miss Goldthorpe were supposed to go for walks or visit places of educational interest. But Wednesday and Saturday mornings when there was nothing to do were few. There were fittings for all Lalla's clothes that were not knitted by Nana. There were walking shoes to be made, and gloves to be bought. Miss Goldthorpe and Lalla shared a dislike for shopping.

"Goldie darling," Lalla would say hopefully, "the sun's shining. When lessons are over, do you think we could go and look at the lock? I think seeing how a lock works is an educational subject, don't you?"

Miss Goldthorpe usually agreed that anything Lalla wanted to look at was an educational subject, because she thought that for Lalla anything that used her eyes and head instead of her feet was educational. But they seldom did the things they planned to do. Presently there would be a tap on the door and Wilson would be there to say that when Lalla had finished her lessons, she and Miss Goidthorpe and Harriet were to go out with her for a fitting for a skating dress. Or Nana would say apologetically, "I don't know what was planned, but I'm afraid you'll have to call in at the shoemakers. They've telephoned to say Lalla's shoes are ready for fitting."

On Saturdays, to make up for the hours when she should have been doing lessons but had spent at the rink instead, Lalla was supposed to work in the mornings. Miss Goldthorpe interpreted the word "lessons," as they referred to Saturday mornings, in the widest possible way. She tried to make Saturday mornings adventure mornings, when the learning took place out of doors. Some days it had been trees and flowers, some days old buildings, and some days following a map. Whatever it was, it was a nice thing to do. There was always a good alternative for indoors in case it rained: special things to look at in museums, pictures to see in a gallery, the under-cover animals to visit at the zoo, or going to Madame Tussaud's.

Lalla's aunt had always known in a vague way about Saturday mornings, but after Harriet joined Lalla for lessons, Aunt Claudia began to steal those precious hours. They suited her. On Saturday mornings she could have Lalla for much longer than the odd hour on Wednesday mornings. She would drive her to Garrick Street, which was in the theatrical part of London, where Lalla's skating dresses were made.

Lalla found Saturday morning fittings an awful bore. She

would stare out of the window at the London traffic while the designer and Aunt Claudia discussed spangles and tutus and pleated chiffon.

At luncheon Lalla would describe these talks to Nana and Harriet. "Goodness, you can't think how awful it was. Talk, talk, talk; jabber, jabber, jabber. I can't think why grown-up people like talking about stuff. The man who makes my frocks showed me some pale blue silky stuff, and asked if I liked it, and I said 'yes.' But, do you know, he and Aunt Claudia talked about it for hours and hours after that."

Miss Goldthorpe went home to lunch on Saturdays, and officially had her Saturday afternoons to herself, though sometimes she stayed on and took Lalla to the rink to save Nana, when Nana had what she called "trouble with her knees." Miss Goldthorpe looked forward to her Saturdays. Often she would go to see one of Shakespeare's plays. There was not always a play in the West End, but there were usually performances that could be reached by bus or tram in some outlying part of London. When there was no Shakespeare for her to see she would either go to a concert or stay at home reading.

Miss Goldthorpe cherished her Saturdays just as anyone treasures a Saturday when he works hard all week, but when she saw Lalla's Saturday mornings being sneaked by Aunt Claudia she was sad, and decided that she must make a sacrifice. She would give her Saturday afternoons to Lalla. After all, she told herself, I'll have my Sundays left, and that ought to be enough for anyone. So one day when she had taken Lalla and Harriet to the rink because of Nana's knees, she caught Max Lindblom's eye and indicated she wanted to speak to him.

"You remember when we planned you should teach Harriet as well as Lalla," she said, "it was because it was good for her.

Now I want you to plan something else which will be good for her." She lowered her voice, for though there was no one near her, she felt like a conspirator in one of Shakespeare's plays planning a dark deed. "I want you to arrange to teach Lalla on Saturday mornings instead of Saturday afternoons."

Max Lindblom was surprised. "But it is nice for Lalla on Saturdays. There are many people there, and after her lesson and her practice are finished, I allow her to dance. Why is it that you wish to change this?"

"Because the shops are shut on Saturday afternoons." Miss Goldthorpe saw he did not follow what she was talking about. "Lalla used to enjoy her Saturday mornings, but lately she has to go to fittings, poor child, and she finds them very fatiguing. You could easily arrange that, couldn't you?"

Max's eyes twinkled. He did not say in words "You and I will plan things together to help Lalla," but he held out his hand and said they were friends, which meant the same thing.

Aunt Claudia agreed to changing Lalla's Saturday skating lessons from the afternoons to the morning.

"I don't quite know why Mr. Lindblom thinks the mornings will be better," she said to Miss Goldthorpe, "but we must fall in with anything that he wants, mustn't we?"

Miss Goldthorpe agreed in a polite way that they must, and began thinking about Saturday afternoons. As a rule Miss Goldthorpe was not a person who pushed for the things that she wanted, but Saturday afternoons were different. It seemed to her terrible that Lalla's life was empty of the sort of things she herself liked best. No music, no plays, not even many books.

Miss Goldthorpe could not imagine a world in which a person did not read. It was not altogether Lalla's fault, she knew, for it was not easy for her to settle down to a book in the evening when she came back from skating. But Miss Goldthorpe was determined that somehow she would get books into Lalla's life; it would be terrible if she grew up with no other interest than skating.

The first thing she did about Lalla's Saturday afternoons was see Olivia. She called on her one day after Nana had taken Lalla and Harriet skating. Olivia was wearing a washing-up smock and asked Miss Goldthorpe to excuse her looking a mess, and to come and sit in the kitchen. Miss Goldthorpe did better than that, she dried the dishes.

"I'm not very domesticated, I'm afraid," she said, "but I can dry dishes without dropping them."

Olivia looked round the kitchen with a disgusted face. "It's been a particularly nasty day. I expect you've heard from Harriet all about her Uncle William. Of course it is not a good time of year, but even so he is sending us the weirdest things. We can't possibly sell them, so we have to eat them. There's no real market, you know, for frost-bitten turnips, nor for apples that haven't kept. Last year he tried an unfortunate experiment with eggs; it was supposed to make them keep longer than most, but it hasn't worked and it's very depressing. Sometimes I open twenty bad ones before I come to one good. I dare say you can smell them."

Miss Goldthorpe had been wondering what it was she was smelling, but she didn't say so, and changed the subject to Lalla.

Olivia was a lovely listener. Even though she was washing dishes she kept turning her face toward Miss Goldthorpe, which showed how interested she was. Because Olivia was so interested, Miss Goldthorpe found herself saying a great deal more than she had meant to say: about how fond she was of Lalla.

"She really is a dear little girl, Mrs. Johnson," said Miss Goldthorpe, "but it's hard for her not to become spoiled because of the way she's brought up. It's made a wonderful difference to her having Harriet to work with her, but I'm afraid that Harriet is inclined to be an admiring audience rather than an outspoken friend."

Olivia washed a saucepan before she answered. "Harriet is naturally a bit carried away by Lalla's glamour at the moment. You see, just now skating is very important to her. Of course she'll never be a skater, poor pet, but you can imagine that to her, being a good skater like Lalla seems a very important thing—which, of course, if you're as good as Lalla, it is. I must say I took quite a different view of skating after I had seen Lalla at that skating gala. The child is really lovely to watch. But I don't think you need worry that Harriet will be nothing but an admiring friend. After all, she's growing up—she'll be eleven this autumn—and she's used to being part of a family who speak their minds."

"Good, I'm glad of that," said Miss Goldthorpe. "But that's not really what I came to see you about. You know the skating's been changed from Saturday afternoons to Saturday mornings?"

"We're pleased. We hardly seemed to see Harriet, and now we can have her on Saturday afternoons."

Miss Goldthorpe leaned against, the sink. "That's what I've come about. I want to make something different of Saturday afternoons for Lalla. Not until after her next skating test, of course, but we ought to make plans. You see, if I don't do something, Lalla is going to grow up knowing nothing at all outside the skating world, which would be really terrible."

Olivia had finished washing the dishes. She let the water out of the sink, dried her hands and put an arm through Miss Goldthorpe's.

"Come into the other room and tell me how I can help. I'll love to do anything I can, and I'm sure together we shall manage it."

Everybody in Lalla's house was gay that spring, because

Aunt Claudia was happy. Now and again Cook muttered to Wilson and Helen that Lalla's diet was all a lot of nonsense, and that for twopence she would send up a nice cake to the schoolroom. Sometimes Nana, especially on days when her knees were bad, complained that Lalla was looking thin (which was not true), but on the whole everybody was pleased and one day slipped into another in a nice way.

It was quite easy for Miss Goldthorpe to persuade Aunt Claudia one Wednesday that it would be a good idea for Alec and Toby to come and give Lalla gardening lessons, and that as the days grew longer they ought to come in the evenings when she came back from skating. Miss Goldthorpe put the request suitably, saying she thought that Lalla would take more interest in botany if she learned it by gardening than if she learned it from a book. Aunt Claudia agreed. Apart from botany she was sure gardening was good for Lalla, because it meant stooping. Aunt Claudia had faith in stooping. She stooped and touched her toes twenty-five times before breakfast every morning to be sure she kept her beautiful waistline.

The two skating galas were as big a success as the first one had been. Lalla got applause; cheers, a bouquet, paragraphs in the papers, and was photographed. Aunt Claudia got envy and nice things said, and a creamy purr and smiling look became part of her.

"We must make big plans for the autumn, Lalla darling. I think little Miss Moore is going to be in great demand, don't you?" she asked.

But behind the ordinary goings-on of the house and the agreeableness of Aunt Claudia there was a little nag of worry inside Harriet. It was surprising what a difference proper lessons from a teacher like Max Lindblom made in her skating. Nobody watched her or saw how she was getting on. She was still at the very early figures, but unlike Lalla, she adored figures. Once she had grasped the tracing her skates should leave on the ice, she did not mind how long she went on working to get it right. Max Lindblom would watch her almost with tears in his eyes. "Look at little Harriet, how she works," he would say. "If only I could make Lalla do that!"

Because Harriet worked hard and loved skating, and because her skating lessons were only provided so that she would be able to take an intelligent interest in Lalla's skating, Max taught Harriet how to do figures that usually he left for a later stage. When he taught her curves he meant only to show her how to do them forward on, the outside and inside edge. But because it might help Lalla, and because she worked so hard, he found himself showing her how to do an outside curve backwards.

Harriet had none of Lalla's verve and gaiety. She worked slowly and methodically so only sometimes did Max realize she was enjoying herself. But once during a lesson he asked if she were tired. She looked up with shining eyes and said that of course she wasn't tired, nobody could be tired skating.

The more she knew about skating the more Harriet worried about Lalla. She was always on the private rink when Lalla was supposed to be practicing her brackets. Harriet could not do a bracket, but Max had drawn her pictures of how they ought to look, and he had done them for her on the ice as well, so that she could see them for herself.

It was all very well for Lalla to look proud and grand and say, "Silly old brackets! You watch me, Harriet, this is how I finished at that gala. I'll show you me taking my bouquet," and imitate herself skating. Harriet knew that never when she watched Lalla do a bracket were her tracings right. They were nearly right, but were they right enough to pass a silver test, which was a very difficult thing to pass? Also she thought Max Lindblom was worried. Often he asked her if Lalla was practicing. It was difficult for Harriet—she did not want to be a sneak and say no, but she did most dreadfully want Lalla to pass her test. Lalla knew for certain that she was going to pass; she had always had everything that she wanted, and now, after her success at skating galas, she wanted to fly through her silver test with the same ease that she had passed her inter-silver.

Harriet hoped that she was fussing for nothing, and that Lalla would pass, because nobody could imagine her failing at anything. But she did wonder when Lalla was going to work to make sure she passed. It seemed odd that she could pass with only trying the figure once or twice in practice, and spending the rest of the time at her jumps and the other sorts of skating that she liked doing.

Sometimes Harriet wondered what would happen to her if Lalla did not pass. She was being given skating lessons, which must cost a great deal of money, because having someone to skate with was supposed to be good for Lalla. If Lalla failed, would Aunt Claudia come up to the schoolroom and say, "Go home, Harriet Johnson, you haven't done any good at all. You can't take lessons with Lalla any more, or go skating, fencing, or dancing with her. Lalla never failed at anything in skating until you came into the house."

As the day of the examination grew nearer, Harriet nearly had a quarrel with Lalla. It would have been a quite serious quarrel except that it was all Lalla's idea, and it takes two people to have a proper quarrel. It started when Lalla was doing an "Axel." Axels were what she called her grandest sort of skating, and she liked doing them and meant to perform them in every free skating exhibition she gave. She was going to do one in her three minutes' free skating for her silver test.

Ever since Lalla had skated in public she had liked an audience. She loathed being made to practice on the little rink. She thought it was much more fun in the middle of the big rink, where lots of people could see what she was doing, but since she was made to practice on the small private rink, somebody had to watch her.

Lalla would have liked to have either Nana or Miss Goldthorpe as an audience, but they were disappointing watchers. Nana was always looking at her knitting at the wrong moment, and saying, "Very nice, I'm sure, dear, but don't slip and hurt yourself." And Miss Goldthorpe would look and say, "Splendid, dear," but as Lalla told Harriet, you could see she was not watching, she was thinking of one of those nasty old plays of Shakespeare's.

As the only audience left was Harriet, Lalla insisted on having her attention. Every few minutes she would call out "Look, Harriet." "Watch this Harriet." "I bet you wish you could do this, Harriet."

It was when Harriet watched Lalla's fourth Axel that she felt she had to say something. "I thought that was awfully good, but oughtn't you to be doing those brackets? You haven't done them yet, and it's only thirteen days to your test. I counted on the calendar this morning."

Lalla knew she ought to be working at her brackets, and though she was certain she could work at them for the last few days, and then do them easily on the test day, she still did not like to be reminded about them. It was such fun doing things fast, and so dull doing brackets and studying tracings. Because she knew Harriet was right and would not admit it, she lost her temper.

"I wish you'd leave me alone. Fuss, fuss, fuss. I'll pass my silver test, but if I didn't it would be your fault. It's very bad to keep worrying a person; Goldie told me that. She said before examinations and things you just ought to forget about them, and then you did much better."

Miss Goldthorpe was not at the rink, but if she had been there she would have been very much surprised indeed to have heard this description of what she had said. Harriet knew Miss Goldthorpe had not said anything to Lalla about not working before her examination, but she did not want to make Lalla crosser, so she said in as nice a way as she could:

"I didn't mean you wouldn't pass. I only meant those brackets are awfully difficult; you told me so. And you are supposed to work at them every day, and today you haven't. I was only reminding you."

Lalla felt angrier than ever. Well, don't remind me any more. I don't want any reminding from anybody, especially not from you. You don't know any more about skating than Nana does, and never will."

Nana, knitting as usual, had been disturbed by Lalla's raised voice, and had heard the last part of what she had said.

"What's that, Lalla? Come over here, both of you."

She waited until they reached the barrier. "What were you saying to Harriet, Lalla?"

Lalla learned on the barrier. "I was telling her to leave me alone. She was fussing at me about my practice."

"And why shouldn't she? Isn't she having lessons with you to see that you work? What were you wanting her to do, Harriet?"

"Brackets," replied Harriet.

Whenever that word was used Nana saw in her mind's eye some brackets that had been in her home when she was a little girl. They had been made of wood, covered in a pinkish plush, and on each bracket stood photographs of her relatives. To Nana one skating figure was the same as another, but she had grasped that brackets, though not made of pink plush, were part of Lalla's silver test, and had to be practiced.

"And Harriet's quite right. I was thinking myself we weren't seeing much of those brackets. Now back you go on the rink, and let me see them right away, or I'll go outside and call Mr. Lindblom and tell him how you're behaving."

As they skated back across the ice Lalla, her temper quite gone, squeezed Harriet's hand.

"'I'm going to imitate you doing curves. As I finish them you are to clap and say what lovely brackets they were."

Lalla was very good at imitating people. Standing ready to start, looking serious, she stopped being Lalla and became Harriet She looked almost as thin as Harriet. Harriet forgot that she ought to be cross with Lalla because she still had not practiced her brackets, and laughed and laughed. It was a very painful sort of laughing, because it had to be done inside where Nana could not see it. Nana watched Lalla being Harriet-doing-curves for a few moments, and then nodded in a pleased way. "Very nice too, dear," she said, and went back to her knitting.

As the day of the test grew nearer and nearer Harriet worried more and more. It was not exactly that she thought Lalla would not pass, but even if she only just passed everything nice might come to an end. Aunt Claudia was sure to say that Lalla was doing worse instead of better since she had known Harriet, and stop Harriet's lessons. That would mean no more fencing, no more dancing and, worst of all, no skating lessons from Max Lindblom. When Harriet thought of that a lump came in her throat. No more lessons from Max Lindblom! It would be the most terrible thing that could happen to anybody.

Soon Harriet stopped reminding Lalla about practicing her figures. For one thing, Lalla was practicing them without being reminded. It was not the sort of practicing Max expected her to do, but she did practice them for a bit, and then dash round the rink in a mad-doggish way, and come back and practice them again for a few minutes. The other reason why Harriet stopped reminding Lalla was because of what Miss Goldthorpe had told her when they were waiting for Lalla to be called for her inter-silver test: that lots of people passed examinations who did not know much, and people who knew a lot sometimes failed. Lalla was the sort of person who passed even if she didn't know a lot. It was better for her to feel confident.

It was noticed at home that Harriet was worried.

"Hullo, Long-face," Alec said.

Harriet flushed, for she did not want anybody to notice she was worried. "I haven't got a long face," she said.

Toby looked up from a sheet of figures on which he was working. "You haven't usually, but lately you've looked as if it had been raining for weeks and weeks."

Edward was lying on the floor, making something out of the Meccano set Lalla had given him for Christmas. "This morning a lady said that seeing me was as good as the sun's coming out," he announced cheerfully.

Alec made a face at him. "One more word like that and we'll drown you. You get more loathsome every day."

Olivia looked at the clock, and said:

"Put that Meccano set away, Edward. I dare say you make strangers think the sun is coming out, but you make me think it's time you were in bed."

Edward gazed reproachfully at Harriet. "If you hadn't looked miserable I wouldn't have remembered what that lady said, and then I wouldn't have been sent to bed for another ten minutes, would I, Daddy?"

George was doing accounts. He murmured, "Two rabbits, ninety-two sacks of winter greens—eight of them too decayed to sell—a crow that probably got in by mistake . . . what was that, Edward?" Then he turned to Olivia. "A crow should cook nicely with a rabbit, shouldn't it?"

"I shouldn't dream of cooking the poor crow. You can give it to the cat up the road, if you like. . . . We were saying Harriet looked worried. Are you worried, Harriet?"

George looked at Harriet. "Seems all right to me. Has the doctor seen her lately?"

Harriet was standing near her father. She leaned against his chair. "Not as a doctor, but in the street. He said I was his walking advertisement," she announced.

George said "Good" and was going back to his accounts, but Toby stopped him.

"All the same, she is looking worried," he insisted. "I suppose it's because she thinks Lalla won't pass that skating test."

Hearing Toby say her worst thought out loud like that made Harriet feel as though she had had the wind knocked out of her. She glared at him.

"Of course I'm not worried. She's going to pass just as easily as she passed her inter-silver, probably better."

Toby shrugged his shoulders. "All right, keep your hair on, but if she's going to pass I don't know what you're getting in such a flap for."

"I'm not in a flap!" shouted Harriet.

Olivia was helping Edward put away his Meccano set. She

smiled at Harriet. "It's natural you should worry for her, darling. Everybody worries when people are going in for examinations, but I'm sure you needn't."

"Of course you needn't," said George. "I thought the child was a genius when I saw her. Passes my comprehension how you spin round like that on a pair of skates. Hard enough to do it wearing shoes."

"Anyway," said Alec, "you haven't long to wait. I wouldn't get into a state if I were you."

Olivia had finished clearing away the pieces of Edward's Meccano set. She stood up and gave Harriet a kiss. "I shall be very glad when that test is over, because Miss Goldthorpe is planning some nice Saturday afternoons for you two this summer."

Harriet was surprised. "Saturday afternoons, but. . . ."

Olivia shook her head. "Don't ask me—it's a secret until after the test—but it's something to look forward to, I promise you that."

Because all the family seemed so sure that Lalla would pass, and Lalla herself felt she would pass, Harriet did worry less, and came to the rink on the test morning feeling not too scared. Miss Goldthorpe was the perfect person to wait with when you were scared of something. She thought it unimportant if Lalla passed or not, though she did realize that other people thought it important, so she was happy and calm. She knew Harriet would not feel calm, though, so she did not bury herself in one of Shakespeare's plays, but talked to her about ordinary things. They were using the big rink for the tests that morning, so part of it was roped off, and on the other half Lalla and the other people going in for tests were practicing. Lalla, as usual, was wearing a short white skirt and sweater, a white bonnet, and white gloves because it was a test. She looked calm and unconcerned, but presently she skated over to Miss Goldthorpe and Harriet. She leaned on the barrier.

"You won't forget about holding your thumbs, will you, Harriet?" she asked.

"Of course not. I was going to, anyway."

Lalla looked at Miss Goldthorpe. "Haven't you anything you can do to bring people luck, Goldie?"

Miss Goldthorpe was just going to say that she did not believe in luck, but believed in knowing your subject before the examination and then hoping for the best, when she saw that Lalla was fidgeting with one of her gloves. Lalla usually never fidgeted, for she was not nervous. Seeing her nervous surprised Miss Goldthorpe and made her sorry, so she tried to think of something which would help.

"I shall sit on my handkerchief. When I was a child I remember hearing an aunt say that when she was playing whist and was having bad luck she would improve it by sitting on her handkerchief. As soon as it's your turn, I shall sit on mine."

"Did your aunt win after that?" asked Lalla anxiously.

Miss Goldthorpe took her handkerchief out of her pocket and said, "Of course. That's why I remember it. It seemed such a simple thing to do."

Lalla hesitated, as if she would like to say something else. Instead she nodded as if she were satisfied, and skimmed back across the ice to her practice.

Half an hour later it was Lalla's turn. There were two judges, as there had been for the inter-silver test. This time they were both women, one plump and one thin. They seemed to know Lalla and greeted her with friendly smiles. Lalla appeared completely at ease, just as she had seemed before she went on for her inter-silver test. She found a piece of ice with no tracings on it and stood calmly waiting to be told to start.

Standing by the barrier, close to where she and Miss Goldthorpe were sitting, Harriet saw Max. His eyes were on Lalla, but he was looking quite at ease, his hands in his pockets. "He doesn't seem fussed," thought Harriet, grasping her thumbs, "so I shouldn't think there's any thing to fuss about."

At that moment Lalla was told to start her first figure, and Max's attitude changed. Harriet saw that his face was grave and that he had clenched his hand in the pocket nearest to her. She turned to Miss Goldthorpe.

"You are sitting on your handkerchief, aren't you, Goldie? It's now."

Miss Goldthorpe patted Harriet's knee. "Of course I am. Don't worry."

Harriet knew more about skating by this time than she had known when she had watched the inter-silver test. But the place Lalla had chosen on which to skate was near the center of the rink, and Harriet could not see the tracings. She watched the faces of the two judges as they stooped down and examined the tracings, and tried to gather from their faces and from the way they wrote on their cards how Lalla was doing. But people like judges, she discovered, did not have faces that told you things. Because Harriet had watched Max giving Lalla lessons, and because for the last two or three days the lessons had been a run-through of exactly what Lalla had to do in her test, Harriet knew when the figures were finished. She let out a gulp of breath.

"She's finished the figures, Goldie. She'll do her free skating presently. She likes that better."

But Lalla had not finished her figures. The two judges called her over and told her something. It was clear from Lalla's way of standing that she was surprised at what she heard; she threw up her head so that her chin was in the air, and clearly was answering proudly. Max moved up so that he was standing next to Harriet.

"It is those brackets. She must do her forward-inside again."

"If she does them right this time, will she pass?" asked Harriet.

Max had his eyes on Lalla. He spoke as if he were talking to himself. "How can she do well if she will not work?"

It seemed as if everybody round the rink was holding his breath. It felt to Harriet as if Lalla took hours and hours to repeat the two figures. When at last she had finished, Max, who was wearing his skates, went across to hear the results with her. The judges seemed to be taking a long time. Harriet, who remembered exactly how everybody had looked when Lalla had got good marks for her inter-silver test, saw that things were different this time. The judges smiled, but it was a different sort of smile this time, and Lalla did not dash over to Max and hold his hands. Instead, she said something quickly which Harriet could not hear, threw her chin in the air and skated towards Harriet and Miss Goldthorpe. As she reached the barrier she said in a be-sorry-for-me-if-you-dare voice:

"It will surprise you to know that Miss Lalla Moore has failed her test."

Miss Goldthorpe said, "I'm sorry, dear. But not by much, I hope."

Lalla looked prouder than ever. "If you want to know, very badly indeed. I needed fifty-four marks to pass, and all I got were forty-one."

CHAPTER 11

Plans

IT WAS AWFUL for Lalla to go home after her test. Miss Goldthorpe tried to talk about other things, but nobody answered. Harriet kept looking at Lalla's face, and answers to Miss Goldthorpe dried up inside her mouth. She was sure that if it had been she who had hoped to pass and had failed, she would have cried, but Lalla did not look a bit as though she might cry. She looked much more as if she might bite somebody. Her face was pink, her lips were pressed together, and she had a very angry look in her eyes. Just before the car reached the house Lalla, still speaking in a proud voice, said:

"No one is going to tell Aunt Claudia instead of me. I know I ought to have passed. It was those silly old judges who were wrong."

Miss Goldthorpe looked worried. Too often in the past she had heard girls blaming the examiners when they did not pass examinations, but she did not say so. It was not the moment to make Lalla feel worse than she was feeling already. Instead she said that of course Lalla must tell Aunt Claudia, and explain that Max Lindblom had said she would try again in the autumn. Miss Goldthorpe and Harriet would go straight up to the schoolroom, and Lalla could find Wilson and ask when her aunt would be in.

Aunt Claudia was not in, but Wilson said she thought she would be in for lunch. Then she looked at Lalla.

"What's the matter, dear? You passed your examination all right, didn't you?"

Lalla was standing on the bottom of the stairs leading into the hail. She swung on the banister rail so that her back was turned to Wilson.

"Actually I didn't, but I ought to have. It was the silly old judges' fault."

Wilson, like everybody else in the house, had got so used to the idea that Lalla was destined for great things in the skating world that she was sure it wasn't Lalla's fault if she had not passed an examination.

"What a shame! But I wouldn't worry if I were you, dear. Skating as prettily as you do, I don't see what you want with any old examination. Look at the lovely pieces in the paper about you."

"You have to do figures, that's the awful part. Do you know, Wilson, I hate, hate, *hate* figures!" Lalla sat down on the stairs. "I shall wait here for Aunt Claudia. I want to get telling her over with."

Wilson knew just how Lalla felt. When she had to tell Aunt Claudia something had gone wrong, she too would hurry to get it over. But being found sitting on the stairs in your outdoor things was not the best way to please Aunt Claudia.

"I know how you feel, dear," she said, "but if I were you I'd run up to Nana and change into something pretty. You know the way your aunt likes you to be dressed. The moment she comes in I'll ring Nana's bell three times."

Lalla got up slowly. "All right. I'd much rather sit here—I

don't want to tell Nana—still, Aunt Claudia would rather I was dressed up, so I'll do it."

Miss Goldthorpe and Harriet had not told Nana that Lalla had not passed, but of course Nana knew. She had asked the moment they had come in, "Where's Lalla?" When they said that Lalla was downstairs waiting to see Aunt Claudia, Nana had made upset, clucking noises, and gone into Lalla's bedroom thinking, "Oh dear, there'll be trouble about this."

When Lalla came in, still looking as though she would bite if anyone spoke to her, Nana said nothing about skating. She took Lalla's coat and hung it up in the closet and was just her usual cozy self. Because she was her usual self and not looking sorry or worried, Lalla stopped feeling angry, and the moment she stopped feeling angry she felt miserable and had to cry. She flung her arms round Nana and sobbed and sobbed.

Nana sat down in an armchair and took Lalla on her knee, and heard, between the gulps and the sobs, that Lalla was shamed for life; that Aunt Claudia would be so angry that she would probably kill Lalla; that she ought to have passed, but it was the judges' fault; that she would be the greatest skater in the world and then they would be sorry.

As the tears grew a little less, Nana heard that Aunt Claudia would say Lalla had not worked very hard—and the awful thing was that it would be true. Lalla hated those old brackets and she had thought she could do them without working. Now, because she had not passed, Harriet would not be coming for lessons any more, and nothing nice would ever happen again.

When at last Lalla finished crying and explaining, Nana stroked the hair away from her face and gave her a handkerchief to blow her nose.

"Now come along and wash. We don't want your aunt to see

you swelled up like that. It would never do. You know, dear, you've been a bit of a madam lately, as often I've told you. You had to know best; you wouldn't listen to that Mr. Lindblom when he said you weren't working at those nasty brackets. But you'll be able to try again, won't you?"

Lalla agreed that she would in the autumn.

"Well then, what are these tears for? 'If at first you don't succeed, try, try again.' "

Lalla choked back a sob. "But I'm not used to trying again. I'm used to doing things right away."

"I know, dear, but pride comes before a fall. Now come along. Let me get you tidied up, and then you run down to your aunt and tell her quietly what's happened, and that you're expecting to do well in the autumn. I'm sure she'll be very nice about it."

Lalla was at her basin turning on the water to wash her face. "You don't think that, Nana, you're only saying it to make me feel better. She'll be awful about it, you know she will." Lalla's lips began to wobble again. "Oh, what will I do if she says Harriet can't come here any more? Harriet only comes here to make me work harder, and now I've failed at my very first test after she's come. I just couldn't bear it if I had to go back to doing things alone again."

Nana was laying a frock on the bed, so her back was to Lalla. Lalla could not see it, but Nana's face was worried. It was only too likely that Aunt Claudia would say that lessons with Harriet were to stop. She had always said that a child like Lalla was best kept by herself, not mixing with other children. Now when they had managed to get Lalla a friend at last, look what had happened. To Nana it mattered nothing that Lalla had not passed her test unless it meant that Lalla would be made to work alone once more.

"Did Wilson say what time your aunt would be in?"

"She just said she'd be in for lunch."

Nana looked at the clock.

"It's only half-past twelve now. She's not often in before one. Do you know what I'd do if I were you? I'd telephone your Uncle David at his office and tell him what's happened, and ask him the best way of explaining things to your aunt. Gentlemen, having business heads and all, are good at knowing how things had best be put." She gave Lalla a little push. "Run along down, dear, and do it right away before he goes out to his lunch. You can tidy for your aunt after."

Uncle David was just leaving his office when the telephone rang. He was going to signal to his secretary to say he was out when he heard that it was Lalla. His cheerful voice came down the line.

"How's the child wonder this morning?"

"Not a wonder any more." Lalla's voice rose in a wail. "Uncle David, I've failed!"

Uncle David laughed. "Failed! Isn't that shattering!"

"I knew you'd laugh, but Aunt Claudia won't. And Nana said I was to ask you the best way to tell her so Harriet wouldn't be sent away."

At once Uncle David grew serious. He had not thought of that. He had been glad that Lalla had Harriet to learn things with and play with, and had not thought of its coming to an end, but now he saw what Nana meant. How best *could* it be put?

"Half a moment, poppet, while I think." He sat down at his desk, the receiver in his hand, and doodled on his blotting paper, which always helped him to get ideas. He drew Lalla on skates. Then he drew Aunt Claudia. As he drew Aunt Claudia he knew suddenly the only thing to make it sure that Harriet was not sent away. He spoke carefully, because it was a difficult thing to explain. "You know how important Aunt Claudia thinks this skating of yours is, and she's brought you up to think as she does. But, of course, skating is really like a game; it's grand to be a first-class tennis player or cricketer, but it isn't wrong for somebody not to want to be first-class."

"But I *do* want to be a first-class skater. I'm going to be the greatest skater in the world," said Lalla.

"Do you think Harriet's going to help you to be that?"

Lalla remembered all the times that Harriet had tried to make her practice. "It wasn't her fault I failed. She tried to make me practice my brackets and I wouldn't," she said honestly.

"Harriet sounds fine. I should think you'd listen to what she said next time, wouldn't you? If I were you, and if Aunt Claudia says that Harriet is to go away, I should tell her that if Harriet goes you don't want to skate any more." He heard Lalla gasp. "Well, it wouldn't be as much fun, would it? It's nearly summer and you don't skate much in the summer anyway. I think you would find that Aunt Claudia wouldn't want you to stop skating, and when she heard you would rather not skate than let Harriet go she would let Harriet go on working with you. In the autumn you could work so hard that you could show her what a help Harriet'd been."

Lalla came back to her bedroom looking solemn. She told Nana what Uncle David had advised. Nana made clucking noises with her tongue against her teeth.

"What a thing to ask a child of your age to say! Don't want to skate any more! Whatever next! Still, you don't skate regular in the summer. Mind you, he's right, there isn't no more reason why you should skate than why I should ride a donkey."

That made Lalla laugh. "Silly Nana! Think of you on a

donkey!" Nana was putting Lalla's frock on. When Lalla's head
came out through the top she was serious again. "Do you know, I
think Uncle David really and truly doesn't think it matters if I
skate. I thought before when he said things like that he was teasing, but I think he really doesn't think it matters. That makes me
feel very peculiar."

Nana buttoned the frock. "He's right, dear; you won't be
eleven till the autumn. There's no reason a child of your age
should be set on anything. Of course, with your father behind you
and your aunt so fond of the skating and all, it's got into you."

Lalla moved to the dressing-table for Nana to brush her hair.
She said thoughtfully:

"I feel the way Alice in Wonderland felt when she fell down
the rabbit hole. I mean, it's like me having fallen down a rabbit
hole and found things were different at the bottom. At the top
everybody knew I had to be a great skater, and at the bottom people like you and Uncle David say it doesn't matter much." Nana's
bell rang three times. Lalla looked at Nana. "I'll make Aunt Claudia let Harriet stay. But you and Uncle David aren't going to make
me think skating doesn't matter, so there."

Aunt Claudia had a lot of afternoon engagements, and had
hurried home for a quick lunch before changing for them. She
had no time to waste, but when she saw Lalla she wanted to hear
how many points Lalla had got in her test.

"Did you do well, darling?"

Lalla, having screwed herself up to confessing, did not waste
time. "Very badly. I failed," she announced.

The word failed made Aunt Claudia flinch as if someone
had thrown a stone at her.

"Failed! But Lalla, that's impossible."

"It was not impossible at all, and if you want to know I

failed badly. They let me have my marks. I only got forty-one, and the reason I didn't pass was that I was bored with brackets and wouldn't work at them. Max tried to make me, and Harriet tried and tried, but I wouldn't," said Lalla, bravely.

Aunt Claudia had come in. thinking what a lovely day it was; she had been happy and she felt now that Lalla was deliberately spoiling everything for her. She believed so in Lalla's skating future that she found it hard to take in what Lalla had said. Failed! Failed badly! Forty-one marks—it was impossible. Everybody knew the child had a brilliant future. Then Aunt Claudia remembered that in the afternoon she was going to a bridge party with some of the people she had persuaded to take tickets for Lalla's first skating exhibition. Since that night they had been interested in Lalla and had asked after her. She had told them that this morning Lalla was to take her silver test, and that she was extraordinarily young to try for it. They had said they hoped she would pass, and she had laughed and said: "I don't think we need worry about that." They were sure to ask how Lalla had done. It made her feel quite ill to think that she would have to admit that Lalla had failed. As she thought of her bridge party her voice grew cold and hard.

"Come into the drawing room. We'd better have a talk about this."

Lalla was frightened by the tone in Aunt Claudia's voice, and it made her sound a little rude. "Talk as much as you like. I've told you what happened, and it's me that minds most, not you."

In the drawing room Aunt Claudia dragged a full description of the figure test out of Lalla. Because she had taken an interest in skating when Lalla's father was learning, as well as in Lalla's practice, she knew more or less what Lalla was talking about. She grasped how bad Lalla's tracings must have been, and she felt convinced that Lalla could have done them perfectly if only she had worked. Obviously something must be done to make her work in future. She had got to get through these tests before she could enter for the open championships, with all the fun and the excitement that those would mean.

"I must see Max Lindblom. You must, of course, have extra lessons so that you pass easily in the autumn, and I must arrange somehow for your lessons to continue throughout the summer."

"You can't. Max goes home to Sweden every summer. He sees his family then," answered Lalla.

"We shall see. Then clearly you're having too many distractions. I was never sure if it was a good idea having Harriet to work with you. I knew what it would be; you'd play about and fritter away your time. I'll telephone to Mrs. Johnson and explain that the arrangement must finish."

Lalla was trembling inside and this made her speak in an extra-loud voice, so that it would not tremble too. "If you do that, I won't skate any more."

Aunt Claudia was as surprised as she would have been if a worm had turned round in the garden and told her to look more carefully where she walked. She repeated in a shocked voice what Lalla had said.

"You won't skate any more!" Then, as the meaning came clear, "Lalla! Child! You don't know what you're saying. That isn't my Lalla speaking. Why, ever since you were a baby you've thought of nothing but skating. Not skate any more! Silly child. Why, you couldn't live without skating."

Lalla had heard what skating meant to her ever since she could remember, but as Aunt Claudia spoke she felt glad to hear it again. It made her feel better than hearing Nana and Uncle David say that it was possible she could give it up. But she was not going to give in about Harriet.

"I only said I wouldn't skate any more if you took Harriet away."

Aunt Claudia had been badly frightened. She had been looking forward for so long to the fun that she was going to have when Lalla was a star that even the suggestion that it might not happen made her feel as if the sun had gone in for ever. She did not want to give in to Lalla, but small though Lalla was, Aunt Claudia could see that she meant what she said. The only thing to do would be to agree that Harriet was to go on sharing Lalla's classes and to speak to Harriet. Harriet must be made to understand that she was only being given the privilege of studying with Lalla if it helped Lalla.

"Come here." Lalla came unwillingly. "Don't look cross, darling. You know I'm only thinking of you. I know what a great gift you have and what a wonderful future you're going to have, if only you work. Everything we've planned is for that. We'll say no more about today as a setback, but we won't let it happen again, will we? We'll just be more determined than ever. . . ." She was going to say "more determined than ever that Lalla should be world champion," but Lalla was sure the quotation was coming and said it for her:

"That my 'square-turn'd joints and strength of limb, will make me a champion grim.' I know I've been a carpet knight today, but I won't be any more if you won't say anything more about Harriet going away."

Aunt Claudia kissed her. "That's the spirit. Now run along up to the schoolroom, it's lunch time."

The rest of that skating season passed quickly. If Max was

upset that Lalla had failed to pass her test, he did not tell her so. In spite of Aunt Claudia's suggesting that Lalla should have extra lessons, he refused to give them to her; in fact, before the season came to an end, he stopped giving her lessons at all. He said she could just enjoy herself on the ice and forget about figures because she was getting stale. In the autumn, when he came back from his two months in Sweden, they would get down to her training and work really hard.

To Harriet Max said: "And you too must work in the autumn. After Christmas you will be taking your preliminary and bronze tests. I think it good that you and Lalla should both be working for tests at the same time."

Harriet was terribly pleased that Max thought she was good enough even to try to pass a test. She had not thought of herself as the sort of skater who would enter for tests. She decided that if she was going to try for them, she was not going to wait for the autumn to start working. The rink would be closed for a month, but right up to the day it closed, and on the day it opened again, she would be there for her usual afternoon practice.

She was surprised that Max thought it a good idea for her and Lalla to work for tests at the same time. Perhaps he did not know that Lalla always wanted an audience, and that you couldn't watch her bracket tracings and practice figures yourself at the same time. Then, of course, Max did not know what Aunt Claudia had said. Harriet had not understood herself everything that Aunt Claudia had said. But she *had* understood how lucky she was to be allowed to work with Lalla, and that in exchange she must see that Lalla passed her silver test in the autumn with almost full marks.

Harriet did not need to be told to want Lalla to pass with high marks in the autumn; she wanted it without any telling, but she did wish Aunt Claudia did not think she could arrange it. Lalla had worked really hard for a bit after she failed in her test, which was why Max told her not to work any more in case she got stale, but Lalla was not the sort of person to go on working like that. If ever she thought she knew a figure and did it well, she would get excited and probably not work again for weeks and weeks.

Luckily that summer lots of nice things happened which stopped both Lalla and Harriet from thinking about skating tests. Miss Goldthorpe's Saturday afternoons were lovely. She arranged trips by river steamer to Greenwich, and in Uncle David's motor launch to places like Windsor and Hampton Court. She took them to Wimbledon to watch the tennis championships, and to matinees of Shakespeare's plays in Regent's Park. Sometimes she invited Alec, Toby and Edward to come too, which she could do without permission because these were her parties.

At first, after she had failed at her test, Lalla did not want to see Toby lest he say something rude, such as "I warned you."

"You can tell him I passed my free," Lalla told Harriet, "but I didn't exactly pass the figures."

Harriet had not had to say anything. Her family were not interested in skating tests. So far as the Johnsons were concerned, Harriet went skating to grow strong and look less like a daddy-longlegs, and Lalla because it was going to be her profession, and that was the end of that.

That summer Alec's dream began to come true. After consultation with Toby he spent the money he had made on his paper round on fruit and vegetables bought at Covent Garden. He and Toby would get up very early and go to Covent Garden on the Underground. They would be there so early that they saw the fruit and vegetables arrive, smelling quite different from Uncle

William's fruit and vegetables. They would watch the stuff un-
loaded and sometimes, when it was carried on a cart drawn by a
pony, Alec would nudge Toby and say: "That's the sort of pony
and cart I'm going to have."

They could not go to Covent Garden every day because getting up so early made them sleepy at school, and Alec terribly stupid on his evening paper round, so that unless he was careful he
put the wrong papers in the wrong letter-boxes. But they usually
managed to go on Tuesdays and on Fridays.

Toby made an arrangement with his father about Alec's fruit
and vegetables. They were sold separately from Uncle William's,
and the money they brought in was put on one side for Alec. Mr.
Johnson found the arrangement worrying at first because he never
could do accounts, but Toby helped him.

"If you have five pounds of Alec's strawberries at two
shillings a pound, and ten pounds of green peas at one and
twopence, and five pounds of broad beans at one and fourpence,
and you've sold all the strawberries except half a pound, all the
broad beans except two pounds and all the peas except one
pound, you have to give Alec twenty-three shillings and sixpence,
and you are holding four shillings and tenpence in convertible
stock. It's quite easy, Dad."

George Johnson never found it easy, but he did see that for
some reason the shop was doing better. Having good vegetables
and fruit on regular days brought people into the shop who might
not otherwise have come, and when they were there, seeing a rabbit hanging up or some trout in a basket made them wonder
whether they could use rabbit or trout. In the same way they
might come in to buy Alec's good green peas and then notice
some unripe peaches which had fallen off Uncle William's wall,
and think, "Well, stewed peaches will make a change."

Of course there were days when what Uncle William sent nobody could possibly buy. He had read somewhere that there was a form of edible toadstool which was nourishing, so several days running he went out with a sack and picked every toadstool he could find. He sent the sacks to George with a note saying "Sort these out. I believe some of them are good for eating; somebody ought to know." George, trusting his brother William, did try to sort the first lot of toadstools but luckily Olivia spotted what he was doing.

"George! Put those loathsome things back in the sack and burn the lot. I should think you've got enough poison there to kill everybody for miles around."

Because more customers came to the shop things were easier for Olivia. Quite often she would say, "Imagine! I've had to buy everything for supper this evening—there was nothing left over. You can't think what fun it is choosing food, instead of cooking what the shop can't sell."

In July Uncle David and Aunt Claudia went to stay with friends in Canada and Nana went to visit her sister in the Midlands. In August Nana and Lalla were going to a hotel on the Isle of Wight, so while Nana was away Miss Goldthorpe moved into the house and took charge.

It was while Nana was away that the exciting thing happened about Lalla's garden. That summer Aunt Claudia had engaged a new young gardener. His name was Simpson and he was not only a good gardener, but a proud one. It had worried him very much to see his best herbaceous border finishing up with tomatoes, lettuces and some ridge cucumbers. He had spoken about it to Aunt Claudia.

Aunt Claudia was not really garden-minded, but when Simpson pointed out that vegetables were not really right in a herbaceous border she could see what he meant. She told Simpson that it was Lalla's garden, but if he could find Lalla another piece of garden that she liked he could arrange an exchange.

Simpson had heard in the kitchen that Lalla was not really keen on gardening, so he planned to offer her a shady little bit of ground behind a laburnum tree which would not show much. It was not until after Aunt Claudia had left for Canada that he saw Lalla to talk about the exchange, and on that day Alec and Toby had come over to plan autumn planting. Toby had a piece of string between two sticks, and while Harriet held one end and Lalla the other he worked out how many strawberry plants the bed would hold, and Alec wrote the number down in a book.

When Simpson came along he said "Good morning" and then stopped in the loitering way of somebody who wants to be noticed and has something to say. Lalla was enjoying herself, and did not want anyone to bother her, so she spoke in her most madamish voice. But Simpson had children of his own and was not going to be madamed by Lalla.

"I spoke to your auntie about veg in my border, and she says if you was agreeable I could give you a bit of earth some other place for you to dig in."

Lalla looked at Simpson despisingly.

"Thank you. This is my garden and it's going to stay my garden. And it's not a piece of earth, it's going to be a strawberry bed."

Simpson had grand ideas for next year; he was ordering many new plants, lots of them tall, and he could see the effect of his bed would be quite spoiled by short things like strawberries. He was just going to speak his mind about this when Toby said:

"What other garden were you going to give her? Could it be something bigger? You see, there's not much acreage here for strawberries, and we had meant to invest in some prize plants."

At the words "acreage" and "prize plants" Simpson looked altogether different. Evidently Lalla had sensible gardening friends. He knew at once that the bit of a bed behind the laburnum would not do and began thinking what else he could spare. He was a gardener who grew vegetables because he must and flowers because he liked them. He had a bright idea. It would be very nice for him if he could have all the herbaceous border, and Lalla's friends would look after a bit of his vegetable garden.

There was quite a long strip of vegetable garden in which he was meant to plant winter greens. He thought growing winter greens a waste of time; cooks never seemed to want to cook them, and they were what he called "messy" if not used.

"If you'd come this way and have a look there's a nice bit I could spare which would be prime for fruit."

The moment Alec and Toby saw the piece of vegetable garden that might be Lalla's, they were thrilled. It was so large a piece that it was almost the beginning of having a market garden, but there was a snag. It would need constant attention from them both, for it was no good hoping that Lalla and Harriet would look after it properly. Alec saw the only thing to do was to take Simpson into their confidence.

"I say, this would be grand. But the thing is that Lalla lets us plant vegetables and things for market, and Mrs. King doesn't know, and if Lalla had a bit like this we'd have to come here quite a lot."

"It would have to be a secret," Harriet explained. "Can you keep secrets?"

Simpson scratched his head. He did not know Aunt Claudia very well, but he knew from the little he had seen of her and from what he had heard in the kitchen that she was not the sort of person to like things done that she did not know about. But gardening was a nice healthy occupation and he could not think Mrs. King would object to Lalla's going in for it with her friends. It would suit him, and after all Mrs. King never came into the kitchen garden, and what the eye did not see the heart didn't grieve after.

"I reckon I can. You won't want to be setting the strawberries yet awhile, and then I suppose it'd be when you're not in school and that. If you tip me off when you want to come, I could get you in by the side gate."

When Simpson had gone the most tremendous measuring went on, and after the measuring Toby worked out a long sum. It was not the sort of sum which anybody else wanted to do. It was in rods, poles and perches. If a piece of land was so long and so wide and in each square foot of it you could plant a strawberry, and each strawberry plant cost so much, how much would it cost to lay out the whole plot? When he had finished they had thought so much about strawberries that to all four of them it seemed as if the strawberries had been planted and were getting ripe.

Toby said, "We must net them. We don't want your capital eaten by birds, Alec."

Lalla saw the beds scarlet with fruit. "And Harriet and I can sneak out before lessons and pick them ready for you to sell."

Alec shook his head. "They'll have to be picked overnight. Harriet will have to bring them home with her. Toby will meet her and help to carry them, while I'm doing the paper round."

Harriet liked the idea of her and Toby staggering home under basketloads of fruit, but she saw difficulties ahead.

"But I go straight home from skating lots of days. What shall we do then?" she asked.

Alec turned to Lalla. "Those days you'll have to pick them, and we'll have to find a way for Toby to come and fetch them.

Nobody must see him take them, or your aunt will think we're stealing her fruit."

"That'll be all right. If I'm working hard at my skating Aunt Claudia won't be cross about anything." Then Lalla bounced because she was pleased. "Isn't it gorgeous! Giggerty-geggerty, fancy me being the one to start the market garden."

Harriet skipped over to Alec. "We ought to do our pledge. Will it be all right as Edward isn't here?"

Alec said he thought it would be, and he linked his little finger into Lalla's. Lalla linked her other little finger to Toby's, and Harriet linked hers to Alec's and Toby's.

Alec spoke in his solemn, growly voice. "We Johnsons and Lalla, but without Edward, swear on the stomach of our uncle never to divulge what has taken place today."

They lifted their hands.

"Guzzle guzzle guzzle, quack quack quack."

# CHAPTER 12

## Loops

HARRIET WAS GLAD when September came. It had been hot and crowded in their part of London in August. Although there were nice things to do because the boys were having holidays, Harriet missed the rink. She tried to practice skating in her head, but it was not the same thing. Because she missed Lalla and skating, and because it was hot, she began to look rather daddy-longleggish again.

Olivia worried about her.

"You're a miserable little scrap, my pet. I don't want you to go backwards; you were looking so much better. I wish you could go away, but the next best thing is for you to be out all day."

Harriet would have liked to help in the shop or in the house, but she was not allowed to do so. When she was not out with the boys she went down to the river and watched the boats go by, and read Lalla's postcards saying how lovely it was on the Isle of Wight, and wished for the term to begin.

The day the rink re-opened her family noticed that she looked different. Edward was the first to mention it. They were having breakfast at the time.

"Harriet's looking like me this morning, not so good-looking but pleased, like I do," he announced.

After everybody had told Edward what they thought of him they looked at Harriet.

"As a matter of fact," said Alec, "you do look as if you'd had a present."

"Nothing came by the post," said Toby. "Not even a postcard from Lalla."

George took a look at Harriet. "Funny. I was worrying because you were so pasty. You've quite a color this morning."

Olivia smiled. "You do look better, pet, and I can't think why, for it's just as hot and just as dusty. Have you children planned something nice for today?"

Toby helped himself to some stewed plums, which they were having to eat with every meal just then, as a lot of unripe ones were coming from Uncle William.

"We're going to the Tower of London, but Harriet won't come because the rink is re-opening."

"Nonsense!" said George. "Of course she must go to the Tower. There's no need for you to start skating till Lalla comes back, Harriet."

Olivia was looking at Harriet. "Would you rather go to the rink? You are a funny child. I should have thought it would be terribly boring for you all alone."

"I wouldn't have thought anybody could want to go round and round on ice," said Edward, "when they could look at the Traitor's Gate."

But Olivia could see that for some reason Harriet would rather go to the rink. "Whatever you might like, Edward, Harriet would rather skate, so that settles it," she said.

Going back to the rink after a whole month of being away from it seemed to Harriet almost the nicest moment she ever remembered. The first person she saw was Sam. She had not seen much of him since she had had her own skating shoes. He gave her a nice welcome.

"Hullo, duckie, here we are again. Sit down, and let me have a feel of those calves. My, my, we are getting on. Whoever would have thought these muscles were the bits of putty I first felt!"

"You promised me I'd have proper skater's legs like Lalla's."

Sam nodded. "So you have, too, and I hear you're making quite a skater."

Harriet stared at him. "Me! Who told you that?"

Sam winked. "A little bird I know. I got a whole flock of little birds in this place; nothing 'appens on this rink but one of them pops along to tell me. How's Lalla?"

"On the Isle of Wight for another week. She won't come here until Max Lindblom comes back. Then she starts training very hard."

" 'Aving another go at her silver, I 'eard. Oh well, many takes a lot of shots at that," Sam said wisely.

"Sam! She's not going to take a lot of shots, she's going to pass this time. She would have last time only . . ."

Sam held up a hand. "Don't tell me, I know. She didn't work. My birds told me about that too. I don't often get a look at her these days, but you tell her from me not to take it too hard if she fails again. Her Dad—one of the nicest men I ever knew—wouldn't have wanted his kid getting in a state about figure skating, I do know that."

Harriet was very fond of Sam, but she thought that kind of talk would be bad for Lalla.

"If you don't mind my saying so, I wouldn't say that to her. It's most important she should pass this time. You see, she's more or less promised her Aunt Claudia she will, and I think if she doesn't her Aunt Claudia will think it's my fault."

Sam let out a great roar of laughter. "That's a good one, that is. It's not a year yet you've been on this ice. I can see you now, being half carried by your Mum down those stairs, and now you tell me it'll be your fault if your friend doesn't get her silver medal. That's good, that is!"

Harriet saw Sam did not understand, so she changed the subject.

"Has one of your birds told you that I'm going in for my preliminary and my bronze after Christmas?" she asked.

"They have. A whole flock of them told me, and some other things too."

'What other things?" inquired Harriet.

"Nothing I shall tell you now. You come to me in two years' time and I'll tell you if they was right."

It took Lalla some time to settle down after being on the Isle of Wight, but when she did settle she worked well. There were days when she was mad-doggish at practice but most days she tried hard and as a result her tracings grew better. One reason why she worked hard was that Aunt Claudia took to popping in unexpectedly to watch her lessons and practice. Lalla might tease Nana about Aunt Claudia, and mimic her, but she was the sort of audience Lalla liked when she was skating. Nobody else watched her in the same thrilled way that Aunt Claudia did. But Aunt Claudia could be strict. "I don't think that was good, Lalla. You held yourself wrongly, didn't you?" she would say. But often it was "Splendid, dear, now all over again. Work, work, that's our motto, isn't it?"

One reason why Aunt Claudia came to watch Lalla was that as soon as she had passed her silver test, Mr. Matthews was arranging for her to give more skating exhibitions. Whenever Max heard the word "exhibitions" he looked most disapproving, but

Aunt Claudia simply did not care. She knew Lalla enjoyed giving skating exhibitions, she knew she liked being Lalla's aunt when Lalla gave skating exhibitions, and provided Lalla passed her silver test, she was not going to let Max spoil their fun.

Harriet always felt awkward and nervous when Aunt Claudia was at the rink, for she was not sure what she was expected to do. She tried at first to watch Lalla, as she supposed she was meant to do, but she found that this was wrong.

"My dear child, what are you mooning about for?" asked Aunt Claudia. "I thought you were having lessons so that you could be a companion to Lalla. Surely there's some little exercise you ought to be practicing."

When Harriet went off and practiced as directed, that sometimes annoyed Aunt Claudia too.

"Funny child, you've no idea how serious you look. You would think you had to work at skating. This is meant to be fun, you know. You've got to enjoy yourself, and enjoy watching Lalla."

One day when Aunt Claudia was at the rink Max beckoned to Harriet to leave the private rink and come outside and talk to him. He sat down and patted the seat next to him. He looked so serious that Harriet, already very subdued by Aunt Claudia, was sure she had done something wrong.

"Harriet, I have decided that you shall take your preliminary and bronze tests when Lalla takes her silver."

Harriet thought of Aunt Claudia's face and had a sinking feeling inside. "I couldn't. Please, I'd rather not. I'm only here to keep Lalla company. You said after Christmas, and then it was only because . . ."

Max spoke in a very sure voice. "You will take them when Lalla takes her silver in three weeks' time, and you will pass them. When you have passed them we will work together hard for your inter-silver, which you will attempt next May. I do not know, but I think it may be that if Lalla passes her silver test this time, she shall make her first attempt at the inter-gold in May. She may not pass, but it is better she should work than waste her time at the exhibitions."

Harriet felt most peculiar in her chest. She pressed the place that felt peculiar with her two hands.

"Max, not the inter-silver. You know I don't know any of the figures. You are only saying that because you think it will be good for Lalla. But however good it is for Lalla, I couldn't take it, I absolutely couldn't."

Max flicked his fingers, a way he had when he wished to dismiss difficulties.

"There are six months for us to work; that should be enough." He turned to face Harriet. "I am very pleased with you. You have talent, my child."

Harriet peered into Max's eyes, trying to make out if he really thought she had talent, or was just saying it to make her think she should go in for the inter-silver to annoy Lalla and make her work.

"You don't mean that, you know you don't. You don't really think I'll be a skater. You know I'm only learning to make my legs strong, and because it's good for Lalla to have somebody of her own age for a friend."

"It is impossible at your age to say how good a skater you will be, but if you progress as you are progressing now, who can tell? But for you it is necessary you should enter for tests. You must gain confidence. You must forget this Aunt Claudia of Lalla's, that you had weak legs and are a companion for Lalla, and must hit yourself like this." Max gave his chest a hearty smack and said: "Me. Harriet. I have a great skating career in front of me."

Harriet laid a hand on Max's knee. "Please don't talk like that, Max. It isn't really the sort of thing I could ever say, and you know it. And honestly, if I did say it and Lalla's Aunt Claudia heard me, I'm sure I wouldn't be allowed any more lessons, or ever to come to the rink again. Only Lalla can say things like that."

Max got up. He made another flicking, dismissing gesture with his fingers. "Me, I do not care what the aunt thinks. I know what I know, and that is what is right for you and what is right for Lalla."

Harriet went back to the small rink. Aunt Claudia was still there watching Lalla practice. She did not seem to have noticed that Harriet had left the rink, but Nana, sitting several seats away from Aunt Claudia, had noticed. She looked up, gave Harriet a little approving nod as if to say "That's right, back again, dear," and went back to her knitting.

Harriet chose a piece of ice as far away as possible from Aunt Claudia and Lalla, and practiced her figure eights and changes of edge. She did them badly, because she was not thinking about what she was doing. "Inter-silver next May!" She couldn't enter, and even if she could, whatever would Lalla say? Lalla was not the sort of person to like her friend's taking the skating tests she had taken.

Presently Aunt Claudia got up to go. It was at a moment when Harriet was thinking about everything but her feet. She was doing a change of edge as Aunt Claudia passed, and slipped and fell. She had no tights, so was wearing long stockings. When she stood up her stockings and pants met; when she fell there was an ugly gap showing a bare leg. Aunt Claudia paused beside Nana. Her crisp, sharp voice rang round the rink.

"That poor child! She doesn't seem to be getting on very

well. Still, I suppose she enjoys herself, and if Lalla likes having her it can't do any harm her learning."

The moment Aunt Claudia was off the rink Lalla flew across the ice to Harriet.

"You are an idiot, Harriet. You know you can skate better than that. I was simply terrified that Aunt Claudia was going to say it was no good having you taught any more, and if she had I couldn't have blamed her." Lalla giggled. "You *would* choose the one moment she's looking at you to fall down."

Nana looked up from her knitting. "That's not the way to talk, Lalla dear. We can't all have the same gifts, and I'm sure Harriet does her best. There's no need to be unkind just because she fell over. She might have hurt herself. You've fallen over plenty of times, and you haven't caught me laughing at you."

Harriet took Lalla's hand and skated round the rink beside her. She spoke in a low voice so that Nana should not hear.

"You'd have skated badly if you'd been me. Max says I've got to take my preliminary and my bronze when you take your silver."

Lalla squeezed Harriet's hand. "Don't worry, they aren't difficult. I'll help you if I can. Anyway it doesn't matter if you pass or not, does it? I mean, no one's expecting you to be a 'champion grim.'"

Harriet swallowed before she answered. "That's not all. If I pass them Max wants me to try for my inter-silver in May."

The enormity of daring to try for the inter-silver, which Lalla had passed only a year ago, made Harriet's voice end in a batlike squeak. Lalla was as shocked as Harriet.

"Inter-silver next May! But you couldn't! Whatever is Max thinking of? I call it mean of him, and I'll tell him so. Poor Harriet, as if you could!"

Although Lalla said it was mean of Max to plan that Harriet should try for her inter-silver in May, inside she was cross and worried. It made things all upside down having Harriet going in for tests. Tests were *her* things and test days ought to be *her* special days. She would not have minded Harriet's taking her preliminary and bronze tests the following spring, for by then Lalla herself would have got her silver and be working for her inter-gold. But it was a different thing letting Harriet take them this autumn so that she could work to take her inter-silver in the spring. Lalla knew Harriet could not pass an inter-silver test, but she did not like to think of her working for it. The fact that Harriet *was* to work for it, if she passed her preliminary and bronze tests, made Lalla absolutely determined that she herself would pass her silver with good marks.

Although she was working extra hard, Lalla found time to look carefully at Harriet's skating, which she had never done before. Harriet was not the sort of skater anyone would think about. She never did things which caught the eye; she was always in some corner, or, when they were on the big rink, in the center, working away by herself, practicing and practicing, and studying her tracings. Lalla made time to look at some of those tracings, and what she saw made her go back to her brackets, feeling surprised. "She'll pass those tests," she thought, "of course she'll pass them." Then her mind added comfortably, "Anybody would pass those easy tests who works as hard as she does."

Inside Lalla was mixed up, one part of her feeling resentful, and another part ashamed of feeling like that. The resentful part felt that Harriet had sneaked up to being good at skating without saying anything about it, and the nice part said, "Don't be silly; you've been watching her all the time; you could have found out how she was getting on if you'd wanted to."

Harriet passed her preliminary and bronze examinations quite easily. She did not get as good marks as Lalla had when she had taken the tests, for she was stiff and lost marks for style. Harriet's passing her tests only interested herself, Lalla, and Max, for nobody else knew anything about them. Miss Goldthorpe was present and knew, of course, that Harriet was taking tests, but when Harriet said: "They're just baby exams, everybody takes them," she believed her.

Something, she had no idea what, made Harriet hide from her family the fact that she was taking tests. She thought it quite likely she would not pass, and she didn't want to come home and tell her family she had failed. They would be nice but she was sure they would say, when she was not there, "Poor old Harriet, let's hope she hasn't ideas she's going to turn into a Lalla." She did not have any ideas like that, and she didn't want anyone to think she had.

Aunt Claudia turned up in time for Lalla's silver test. She stood as near the judges as she could, looking smart, proud and disdainful. The judges, a man and a woman, did not seem to know she was there, which Harriet thought must be very annoying for Aunt Claudia. The moment Aunt Claudia arrived, Miss Goldthorpe and Harriet moved as far away from her as possible. Miss Goldthorpe sat on her handkerchief and Harriet held her thumbs. This time the thumb-holding and the handkerchief worked. Lalla passed. But only just. Once again Max managed to get her marks: she needed fifty-four to pass and what she got was fifty-five point two. Aunt Claudia was so glad that Lalla had got what she called "that silly test" behind her that she did not mention Lalla's low markings.

"Don't worry, dear. I dare say those judges—what curious clothes—are not very experienced. You've passed and that's what matters. You will, of course, have to work hard at those figures; they must be perfect by the time you enter for open championships, but I'm very pleased with you."

In spite of all Max felt about it, Lalla gave four skating exhibitions that Christmas. He had an argument with Aunt Claudia, but he lost. He arrived at Aunt Claudia's side when she was watching Lalla practice, in a mood to speak his mind; but when it came to mind-speaking it was difficult to be as good at it as Aunt Claudia. She heard what Max had to say about the exhibitions being bad for Lalla, who was not a child whose work was improved by applause and that he wished her to work for her inter-gold only and not be distracted, with an amused expression in her eyes.

"My dear man, there's nothing to get excited about. All work and no play is bad for any child. Lalla is now eleven, and it is important that she gets used to public appearances. It will not be long before I shall be traveling with her all over the world for open championships, as indeed so will you. I never interfere with your skating lessons, but about these public appearances you will please allow me to be the better judge."

Max took a deep breath, and opened his mouth. It was as if he were trying to say something important, and yet was afraid of saying it. Then he shut his mouth, shrugged his shoulders and walked away.

That Christmas Aunt Claudia and Uncle David again went away and Lalla spent Christmas Day with the Johnsons. On Boxing Day she was allowed to invite the Johnsons to her house, to take part in scenes from "Alice."

Lalla played lots of parts. She was the Red Queen. She was the White Knight riding on her rocking horse, and she was the Caterpillar. Lalla was very funny; the audience of Olivia, George,

Cook, Wilson, Helen and Nana laughed and laughed. Lalla's gift for mimicking people made her feel she was the person or creature she was acting. She knew just the right way to say Lewis Carroll's words to make them sound as funny as they truly were. As the Caterpillar she had been sewn by Miss Goldthorpe into a green eiderdown, and her face, looking out, with the hookah hanging from her mouth, was almost as funny as the words. When she had climbed off the piano stool which Nana had trimmed as a toadstool, and crawled out of sight, Cook said:

"She is a caution!"

"Better than going to the pictures," Wilson agreed.

Olivia turned to Nana. "I never knew she was an actress, bless her."

Nana thought acting "Alice in Wonderland" in the drawing room at home at Christmas was the very thing for Lalla to be doing and she was pleased Lalla had made a success of it.

"She was always a rare mimic. Of course I stop her at once if she starts it, but you ought to see the way she takes off her aunt. The very image of her, she is!"

When Christmas was over, there was the excitement of Lalla's four galas. Lalla enjoyed these more even than she had the year before, because now that she was eleven she was not sent home after her performance. Instead she stayed till the end, sitting beside Aunt Claudia, hearing the nice things people had to say about her.

Aunt Claudia too enjoyed Laila's exhibitions more than ever. It was fun having Lalla with her; there was no doubt that she was not only attractive to look at, but had the sort of personality that made people remember her. She was usually amusing and gay, but when she was on the ice to give an exhibition, she seemed to be saying "Look at me, isn't it lovely to be me? I find skating such fun." After the last of Lalla's public performances, Aunt Claudia said as she kissed her good night:

"I'm so proud of you, dear. Do hurry up and pass all those nasty tests, so that you can be entered for open championships. We shall have such fun. We'll take Miss Goldthorpe with us and Nana to look after your clothes, and Max Lindblom. Won't it be exciting?"

Lalla, carried away by the success of the evening and Aunt Claudia's enthusiasm, did something very unusual. She flung her arms round Aunt Claudia, gave her a hug, and said, "Won't it be? I just can't wait."

After that night things began to go wrong. First people at Lalla's house had influenza, and then at Harriet's. When everybody got over influenza, the weather turned bitterly cold. Though the rink was warm and they wore plenty of Nana's knitted underclothes, both Lalla and Harriet got cold and stiff if they stopped working for a moment. Miss Goldthorpe and Nana got chilblains and colds from sitting at the rink, and were inclined to be snappish in consequence. Worst of all, Lalla's skating went wrong.

This time the going wrong was not because Lalla would not work. For her inter-gold she had to do figures called change-edge loops. Change-edge loops needed the sort of skating which was not Lalla's. They needed control and rhythm, both of which she had sometimes, but they needed immense concentration as well, and that was not a quality Lalla possessed when she was skating figures. Somehow, however hard she fought to stop it, her mind would slip off what her feet were doing, and this showed on the ice in a bad tracing. Always before she had been sure she could do a figure if she worked at it, but this time she had to learn a figure she simply could not get right.

Max was sorry for her, as well as worried. "You must relax,

Lalla. This is not difficult for you, you know how it should be; but each day those tracings are worse." He knelt down on the ice and pointed to her circles. "Look at this! And this!"

Lalla became unusually silent for her, and inclined to be sulky.

"I can't help it. I try and try. I don't know why I can't do this stupid old figure. I wish you'd leave me alone."

Max did not mind her sounding cross, because he understood it. "You must not worry, Lalla. We will leave the loops for two or three weeks. If when we try them again they are still difficult, we will give ourselves longer. You will not try for the inter-gold until the autumn."

"I'm trying for the inter-gold this May. I know how to do the beastly things, and you know that I always do better in tests than in practice."

Max nodded, and agreed this was true. He insisted, though, that if Lalla could not get better tracings after a rest she had better leave the test for the time being.

Lalla did not give up her loops. She had no lessons in them for two weeks, but she never stopped practicing them, until at last she began practicing them in her sleep. Sometimes she would wake up with a jump, thinking she had just finished a loop and done it wrong; sometimes she just went on practicing in her head all night. Whichever way it happened, it was bad for her, and instead of looking round-faced and gay with shining eyes, she began to look thin and pale. Her curls hung lankly, and she had a hang-dog look in her eyes. Miss Goldthorpe and Nana were very worried.

"I don't know what it is, Miss Goldthorpe dear," Nana said. "Of course there's this taking the examination again, but then there's always one of those. Last time it was the brackets bothered her. This time, from what I can gather, it's something called the circles; but she's not one to let skating get on her mind."

"Is it her diet?"

Nana made scornful, clicking noises. "Diet! Me let a child in my nursery diet looking the way she does? If there's anything she fancies to eat, she has it, and as much of it as she likes, and has done so ever since she had the influenza. Not that she eats as she should—only picks at her food—and if there's a thing I can't abide, it's seeing a child pick at her food."

"You know Mr. King better than I do; could you talk to him?"

Nana was knitting a new pattern of a sweater, and had to count her stitches. In the pause she thought about Uncle David.

"What would I say? I dare say he'd get Mrs. King to have the doctor along, but he'd only give her a tonic same as he did after the flu."

"Couldn't you get Mr. King to have a talk with Lalla? She's fond of him. And he might get to the bottom of what's troubling her."

Nana considered it. "Well, of course, I always say it's better going to a gentleman when you want advice. Seem to have more sense than a lady. I might do that. She doesn't see much of him really, but it was him that told Lalla to speak her mind about having Harriet to work with her." She turned over the problem a little longer. "I'll do that, Miss Goldthorpe, I can't say when—me not going much in their part of the house—but I'll manage it somehow."

"And I'll have a talk with Max Lindblom," Miss Goldthorpe said. "I'll see him sometime when the children aren't there, and ask whether there's any need for her to take that examination just now. Then I might have a talk with Harriet's mother. She's a very sensible woman, and might have an idea of what's upsetting the child. Harriet may have said something."

Nana shook her head. "Never. Harriet's Miss Quiet in my nursery—you never know what she's thinking. But you see Mrs. Johnson, dear; it can't do any harm and it might do good. Anything's worth trying. It properly upsets me to see my blessed lamb the way she's looking now."

# CHAPTER 13

## The Quarrel

MISS GOLDTHORPE SAW Max Lindblom one evening. He was giving a lesson when she reached the rink, but she waited until he had finished, then asked him if he could spare a moment.

"This is nothing to do with me, and I don't know what Mrs. King would say if she knew I was seeing you, but Lalla isn't herself at all. She's quiet at her lessons, which is quite unlike her, and she gets cross easily, and that's unlike her too. She always was a child who liked to have her own way and order people about, but she never does that now. I almost wish she would. You know, I think this examination is worrying her."

Max did not answer at once. He led Miss Goldthorpe to a seat where nobody could hear what they were saying.

"I do not wish her to try for this inter-gold test," Max began. "There is no need; she is still very young. Why should there be this rush?"

"I think she wants to get it over and done with. You know what great plans there are for her when she has finished with these tests."

Max made an angry, growling noise. "It has been wrong from the beginning. The child has talent, yes. She has a good personality, yes. But these things do not necessarily make the great skater."

"I couldn't agree with you more. I think it wretched that she feels that she must be a skater and nothing else. But she has been brought up to believe in a great future ever since she was a baby, and except of course for that one time when she failed a test, it's all been coming true. But now I gather there is something she can't do. I learn from Harriet she's working terribly hard, and still she can't do whatever it is."

"She will do it, but not yet. The aunt should forbid skating for many months. 'Let us forget it,' she should say, 'let us go away.' You, I think, should tell the aunt to say these things."

Miss Goldthorpe sighed. What a foolish young man he was!

"Mr. Lindblom, I've told you before it's quite impossible for me to say anything like that to Mrs. King. Last time when you asked me to say something to her I explained that if I did it would mean that I would be given notice, and I have no intention of being given notice. I'm not a vain woman, but I do think that I'm useful to Lalla, and I therefore would do nothing to risk offending Mrs. King."

Max shrugged his shoulders. "Then nothing can be done. I have told Lalla she should not attempt her inter-gold this spring."

"Have you told Mrs. King?"

Max lit a cigarette. "The trouble is Harriet."

Miss Goldthorpe's eyes opened very wide.

"Harriet! What has Harriet got to do with it?"

"Skating is a very expensive thing. To work properly you must have what Lalla gives Harriet: the good governess like yourself, the outside classes, everything specially arranged to fit in with the training. It is impossible to train properly and to attend a school. If I say to Mrs. King give Lalla six months, and no skating, that will mean six months without lessons for Harriet."

Miss Goldthorpe switched her mind from Lalla to Harriet. Harriet was stronger now; in spite of influenza and the cold winter she seemed well. She was always frail looking compared to Lalla, but that did not mean she was delicate.

"I don't think you need worry about Harriet. Of course skating has done wonders for her, poor child, but she's much stronger now and she could practice if she wanted to. Mr. Matthews, you know, very kindly lets her come here free of charge."

Max looked pityingly at Miss Goldthorpe, as if he were thinking: "How can I make this poor, ignorant woman see what is so clear to me?" Then he saw that his next pupil was waiting. He got up, said good night, and went back on the ice.

It was a nasty night, with driving rain. Outside the rink Miss Goldthorpe put up her umbrella and walked towards her bus stop, but before she reached it a gust of wind caught the umbrella and turned it inside out. While she was struggling with it she felt it being taken from her hands, and when she blinked away the rain which was in her eyes, she saw that her rescuer was Alec. Alec had the bag which had held papers over his arm, for he had just finished his evening round.

"Hullo, Miss Goldthorpe, were you coming to see us?"

Miss Goldthorpe had been thinking of nothing but how nice it would be to sit in front of a fire and read a book, but now that Alec suggested it, she saw that this was the obvious moment to call on Mrs. Johnson.

Miss Goldthorpe got a lovely welcome from the Johnsons, especially from Harriet, but Olivia guessed she would not have come to see them on a nasty wet night without some reason. She told Toby to take Miss Goldthorpe's wet coat and umbrella and put them in the bathroom, and when she saw George pushing a chair up to the living room fire she stopped him.

"Miss Goldthorpe is staying to supper with us and I'm going to ask her to help me cook it. I'm afraid it's a poor feeding night. March never seems a lucky month for William."

George was not going to stand for hearing his brother William run down. "You can't say that," he protested. "There were five duck's eggs yesterday as well as all those splendid winter greens."

Toby looked up from his homework. "People don't come to us for duck's eggs, and the greens weren't splendid—the Brussels sprouts had gone bad."

Harriet was playing Casino with Edward. "There were some turnips as well. I saw Mummy washing them."

Edward looked reproachfully at his father. "You can say what you like about Uncle William, but nobody can't say that soup, soup, soup every evening is nice—and that's what we have to eat—made with his old vegetables. A lady said to me today I was looking pale, and I told her that was because I ate too much soup."

Olivia laughed. "What nonsense! You don't look pale and you don't have soup every evening, and you know it. As a matter of fact tonight it's curried duck's eggs and vegetables, and you know you'll like that. Come along, Miss Goldthorpe, don't listen to these grumblers."

In the kitchen Olivia shut the door and gave Miss Goldthorpe a chair while she went about her work. The kitchen-dining-room was so cozy that in no time Miss Goldthorpe had told Olivia all about Lalla; how worried she and Nana were, of how she had seen Max, and what he had said.

Olivia had by this time boiled the duck's eggs hard; she gave them to Miss Goldthorpe and asked her to take off their shells.

"It seems to me a lot of fuss about nothing. If it were one of my children I wouldn't let them go near a rink again if I thought it was worrying them. But I suppose Lalla is different. As they are determined to make a skater of her, I suppose she has got to pass these wretched tests. Is there no one who can make the child see it's silly to go in for it now, as her instructor thinks she shouldn't?"

Miss Goldthorpe carefully shelled an egg, then said:

"Having to tell her aunt that would seem to Lalla as good as admitting that she is not the success she's expected to be."

Olivia gave her curry sauce a savage stir.

"If only I could speak my mind just once to Mrs. King. I'm a mild woman, but you'd be surprised what I would say."

"I wouldn't. I've never really lost my temper; it has never seemed worth while. But, do you know, sometimes when I think of the way Mrs. King has brought up poor Lalla I wish I could whip her. Extraordinary, for I don't hold with corporal punishment."

"What about Mr. King? George says he's nice; can't he do anything?"

Miss Goldthorpe explained that Nana was seeing him, but how difficult it was for him to interfere. Then she said:

"I wondered if you would see Lalla. I've been planning a treat for her on Saturday. I've taken seats for a musical entertainment; the advertisements say it's funny. I was not inviting Harriet as I know you like to have her on Saturday afternoons, and from what I read this comedy couldn't do her any good educationally. . . . I wonder, would you use my seat and take Lalla, and have a talk with her? It would be a great kindness."

"Bless you, of course I will. I shall enjoy it. I love musical comedies, and hardly ever get a chance to see one. And of course I'll talk to Lalla, but I don't know if I can help. I haven't seen her for weeks, what with influenza and the foul weather, and last time

I saw her she was on top of the world. I can't imagine that child except on top of the world."

"That, I think, may be the trouble; she can't imagine herself in any other place."

Miss Goldthorpe was a poor liar. On Saturday, in the car driving to the theater, she told Lalla a halting story of a book she had to return, and of how, as Mrs. Johnson was in the West End, she was using Miss Goldthorpe's seat. Lalla laughed at her.

"It's no good telling me that, Goldie. Harriet's mother never would be in this end of London on a Saturday with all of them home, and you know it. I bet it's just you so hated to see a musical comedy you gave your seat away. Isn't that it?"

Miss Goldthorpe was glad Lalla had hit on something near the truth.

"Well, dear, I don't like musical plays."

Lalla put her arm through Miss Goldthorpe's and rubbed her cheek on her shoulder.

"And you paid for the seats. You didn't dare tell Aunt Claudia this was educational, did you?"

"It was a little present for you."

Lalla hugged Miss Goldthorpe's arm closer.

"Dear Goldie, you're an angel, and however much a beast I seem, I truly love you."

Olivia was shocked at Lalla's appearance. The round, gay, bouncing Lalla she knew had disappeared, and in her place was a thinner, almost serious Lalla, with most of the bounce gone out of her. Olivia was thankful to find that the gayness was not quite gone, for the play was very funny and Lalla not only got bouncing and gay from laughing, but in the intervals made Olivia laugh by her imitations of the actors. Miss Goldthorpe had arranged that Olivia should take Lalla home in a taxi, but Olivia thought a taxi would be too quick a journey for her and Lalla to have a proper talk.

"How about our going home on the top of a bus?"

Lalla was charmed. "Could we? Do you know, I've hardly ever been on a bus. Aunt Claudia is afraid of germs."

Olivia looked pityingly at Lalla. Poor lamb! Even a bus was a treat. If only she could steal Lalla and take her home with her.

Olivia was not a mother who asked her children to tell her things. She tried to make them feel she was always interested in anything they would like to tell her, but if they did not want to talk about something, that was their own affair. Because of this, it was difficult for her to make Lalla talk, but in the theater she had planned a way to do it. She started by telling her she was thinner, and asking if it was her diet. When Lalla explained that the dieting had finished, Olivia said she wondered if Lalla was outgrowing her strength, which was something which easily happened at her age. "It happened to me," she went on. "Do you know, I was nearly as tall as I am now when I was not much older than you are."

"But I'm not much taller, only thinner."

"It's the same thing. It means using a lot of energy in growing up, and then there isn't as much energy for other things. I was brought up in South Africa, you know, and riding was my delight. I loved horses more than anything else in the world, and was supposed to be a marvelous horsewoman, but outgrowing my strength affected my riding. I suppose my horses could feel I wasn't as full of pep as usual."

Lalla looked suspiciously at Olivia out of the corners of her eyes. Had Harriet told her about how she could not do loops? Olivia did not look like somebody saying something on purpose. In fact she had stopped talking about outgrowing your strength and was talking about the funny man in the play. Lalla joined in and soon was acting for Olivia most of the parts, and they were both laughing again at the jokes. But underneath what she was saying, and underneath her laughing, Lalla knew something nice had happened. It was as if there had been a tight, hard hand round her middle, and somehow Olivia had loosened it and made her feel better. Presently she asked a question.

"What did you do for outgrowing your strength?"

"Saw a doctor. He cured me."

At Lalla's gate Olivia kissed her good-bye. "I have enjoyed my afternoon. I wish sometimes you could arrange for Miss Goldthorpe to give us another afternoon out."

That night Lalla slept really well. As she was slipping into sleep she thought "How silly I've been. It isn't that I can't do those loops. It's merely that I need a tonic. I'll tell Nana to buy me a bottle." And then, cozily, "And if she won't, Harriet's mother will. It's nice going out with Harriet's mother. I hope I'll be allowed to do it again."

There were no secrets between Miss Goldthorpe and Nana, so Lalla had told Nana about the matinee. At breakfast the next morning she told her what Olivia had said about outgrowing her strength. Nana tried not to look ruffled, but inside she felt it. She might tell Miss Goldthorpe something ought to be done about Lalla, but that did not mean she wanted Lalla asking for a bottle of tonic. Children should not think about their health; that was for grownups to do for them. Then she looked at Lalla and her heart softened. Harriet's mother had done her good. She seemed much more herself this morning, and was eating a good breakfast without being told.

"That tonic was for the influenza and wouldn't do good for anything else. You'll have to see the doctor."

Lalla helped herself to honey.

"I wish I could see Harriet's doctor. Ours is so old and grumpy. Harriet's said she would get well if she skated. I should think a doctor who said that would know something gorgeous to make you stop outgrowing your strength."

After breakfast Nana saw Uncle David walking up and down the lawn smoking. Nana was not fond of gardens in early March, but it was a lovely morning and a good moment to catch Uncle David alone, for Lalla was working in her garden, and Aunt Claudia was still in bed. Nana dressed as warmly as if it were a cold day in midwinter, and went out.

Uncle David was glad to see Nana because he had just been talking to Lalla, and was thinking about her. He said:

"That child of yours has been looking under the weather lately. What are you doing to her?"

Nana glanced up at Aunt Claudia's windows to be sure they were shut.

"That's what I've come out about, sir. She's got another of those examinations coming on for the skating. Mr. Lindblom doesn't want her to take it, but Lalla won't be put off."

Uncle David made a despairing gesture with his shoulders. "Blast that skating! But I can't do a thing unless Lalla asks me to. If I interfere on my own I shall be eaten alive, not only by Mrs. King but by Lalla, and I'd lose the child's trust as well."

"I know, sir. But it seems Mrs. Johnson has told Lalla she might be outgrowing her strength. Not that she is, but thinking it might be that seems to have cheered her up. Childlike, she fancies a bottle of medicine would put her right, and she's taken to the idea that she would like to be given it by the doctor who looks after Harriet."

"You think it would be a good idea?"

Nana did not think it a good idea that Lalla should want to see a doctor. If Nana had her way she would have suggested a fortnight by the sea at Easter.

"I don't know what to say, sir, I'm sure. I try to treat her as I'd treat any child, which is what her mother would have wished, but with the skating and all I can't. Maybe if she's taken a fancy to Harriet's doctor it can't do any harm, though I doubt it does any good."

Uncle David smiled sympathetically.

"Don't worry too much. I'll have a talk with her and try and find out what's on her mind."

Lalla, as instructed by Alec, was raking between the rows of strawberries. The March wind had put color into her cheeks and the good smell of growing things coming out of the earth made her eyes shine, but she still did not look as she ought to look. Uncle David's eyes twinkled when he saw what she was doing.

"You know, poppet, I'll never believe you planted those strawberries. I bet Simpson put them in."

Lalla leaned on her rake. "You're wrong. He didn't."

"But neither did you."

Lalla gave an imitation of Nana. "'Those who ask no questions won't be told no lies.'"

Uncle David laughed. "I've just seen Nana. I told her you looked as if she was starving and beating you, and she tells me you think Harriet's doctor would be the one to cure you. Is that right?"

Lalla laid down her rake and joined Uncle David. "Yes."

Uncle David took her hand. They walked down the path. "What's the matter with you?" Uncle David asked.

Before yesterday afternoon Lalla would not have answered that, but now, certain a bottle of tonic from the right doctor was all she needed, she explained about the loops that would not come right; how she even tried to do them in her sleep; how fussed she had been. Now that she knew that nothing had gone wrong with her skating, but that it was only outgrown strength, she was not worrying any more.

Uncle David watched Lalla while she talked. She was not big for somebody of eleven; in fact she was short for her age. He doubted if any doctor would think outgrown strength was the trouble.

"I expect you've been overworking. Isn't the child wonder taking another skating test?"

"Yes. The inter-gold in May."

"I dare say the doctor will suggest less tests. It's a way they have."

Lalla stood still, all the pink made by the wind leaving her face, and the gayness disappearing from her eyes.

"Then I won't see him. I've got to pass that test, absolutely got to."

"Why this May? Wouldn't next year do?"

Lalla tried hard to explain.

"No. It must be now, so I know I can do it. If I have to wait I'll think and think I can't. And I simply couldn't bear that."

Uncle David gave her a friendly pat on the back.

"What rot! You know you and your aunt between you are making martyrs of yourselves for this skating; simply couldn't bear it because you might be told not to take a test for a month or two. Really, Lalla!"

Lalla kicked a stone off the path.

"Silly Uncle David, you don't understand." Lalla's voice wobbled. "It was awful that time I failed my silver, more awfuller than anybody knew. People looked sorry; nobody had ever looked sorry for me before and I hated it. When people look at me without looking proud of me I feel I'm not Lalla Moore any more."

Uncle David lit another cigarette. He lit it very slowly to give him time to think of what he had better say.

"It sounds as though we must try and fix it for this doctor of Harriet's to give you a bottle of champion-skater mixture, if that's what you want. But you've got your ideas all upside down. The Lalla I know is an amusing child, and I believe could make her mark in the world without ever putting skates on again. There's a saying, 'There are more ways than one of killing a cat,' and I think there are more talents than one belonging to Lalla Moore, but I know neither you nor your aunt will believe it."

Uncle David knew it was impossible to get Aunt Claudia to agree to Lalla's seeing a new doctor; he would be asked what Lalla's doctor had to do with him. Aunt Claudia usually left Lalla's health to Nana, and sent for the doctor only when Nana asked her to. She might have noticed Lalla was looking peaky and be thinking of her seeing the doctor, but she certainly would not want Uncle David to suggest it. The only thing to do was to ring up Olivia and ask her to arrange it.

Olivia did arrange it. She saw Doctor Phillipson and told him all about Lalla, and he and she made a plan. It was arranged that the next Saturday Miss Goldthorpe, instead of taking Lalla to a theater, should take her to see a local film, and afterwards they would have tea at the doctor's house.

That next Saturday Miss Goldthorpe talked to Mrs. Phillipson in the drawing room while Dr. Phillipson talked to Lalla in his office. He explained it could be only talking; Lalla was not his patient, but he might find out what sort of medicine she needed just by talking. He was, Lalla found, easy to talk to and enormously interested in skating. He wanted to know all about her training from the very beginning, all about tests and what you had to do at them. To make figures clear to him Lalla drew them for him. The last figure she drew was loops.

"These are what I have to do in May and they've been going wrong. So that's why Goldie brought me to tea, because I was sure a man like you who thought of skating to cure Harriet's legs being wobbly would know what to give me for outgrown strength which makes my loops go wrong."

Doctor Phillipson seemed to be studying Lalla's drawings. Inside his head he was wondering how best to help her. After a bit he sat down, took a piece of notepaper and began writing.

"I can't guarantee this, but have it made up, take it regularly, and it might do the trick!'

Lalla looked at the sheet of paper. Most of it she couldn't understand for it was written in doctor-writing, but at the top was printed in big letters, "SKATING MIXTURE FOR LALLA MOORE. ONE TABLESPOON TO BE TAKEN DAILY BEFORE VISITING RINK."

The medicine worked. Lalla felt better and worried less, and so her loops were better. Then, so slowly she scarcely noticed it, the effect of the medicine began to wear off. Max Lindblom could have explained that if she was judging the medicine by her loop tracings it was bound to stop helping her, for her loops were as good as she was going to get them for the present, and no medicine would make them any better. But Lalla had not told Max about the medicine. She wanted him to think she did her loops marvelously without help, so when they stopped getting better she could not talk to him or anybody about it, but just felt more fussed and bothered than ever all by herself. Everybody was sorry for her, but nobody knew how to help her.

"She's like a reel of cotton come unfixed in a work basket,"

Nana said. "Tied into knots round everything. You don't know where to start to look for an end to start rewinding."

Aunt Claudia was as bothered about Lalla as everybody else, but her bothering over her got Lalla into a worse state. Aunt Claudia thought Lalla was suffering from quite unnecessary nerves.

"Cheer up, dear, it's not like the Lalla Moore I know to worry. Where's that champion grim got to, I wonder?"

Lalla usually refused to answer, but sometimes she would be rude. "Don't talk like that! I'm not a baby."

That would make Aunt Claudia try to be especially understanding. "Of course you aren't. Eleven and a half is a big girl. Don't think I mind for myself if you're a little rude—I know that's just a sign that you have temperament, and a skater must have that—but my Lalla mustn't forget a great skater has also to be her country's ambassadress."

Once Aunt Claudia suggested that perhaps Lalla should see the doctor. "You're getting thin, darling. Perhaps the doctor would give you something to make you fatter."

"My goodness! I thought you wanted me thinner. All those months no potatoes, no cakes, no nothing nice. Now you want me to see a doctor because I've got thinner. Well, I won't see him, so there. I'm not Alice in Wonderland eating things all the time to make me grow littler and bigger."

Aunt Claudia did not mention a doctor again to Lalla; but she did to Nana. "I think Lalla ought to see a doctor. She seems a little nervous, but I won't worry her until after her test."

Nana said politely "Just as you say, ma'am," but her tone showed that she did not think much of what Aunt Claudia had said.

Aunt Claudia was not particularly worried about the test, because she did not know how Lalla was doing. The moment the effect of the medicine began to wear off, as Lalla thought, she told Aunt Claudia she was not to come to the rink. Nana heard Lalla tell Aunt Claudia this and was terribly shocked.

"A child your age speaking that way to your aunt! You won't have her coming, indeed! The nursery is now the schoolroom, but from the sound of you it ought to be my nursery again. I'd teach you how a little lady ought to behave."

Aunt Claudia was shocked too, and also hurt.

"Not come! But you know how I love watching you skate. And now that we are nearing the time when you can enter for amateur championships you must get used to me watching you. Just think, Lalla! If you get your inter-gold this time, there is only the gold left, and then our fun starts. But it's our fun; we're going to share your triumphs, aren't we?"

Lalla's inside felt as if it were rolling over. Inter-gold this time! "Only the gold left! . . . Share our triumphs!" If only it was happening. It had got to happen. Somehow she would pass her inter-gold, and then Aunt Claudia would never know she nearly had not been able to do loops.

"I don't want you to come until I ask you."

"But why not, dear?"

"Because I don't." Lalla remembered how she had made Aunt Claudia let Harriet go on sharing classes. "If you come, I won't skate—I'll go home."

That settled that. Nana opened the door for Aunt Claudia and saw her downstairs. When she came back her face was red.

"That I should hear a child of mine speak that way. It's not altogether your fault; you've been brought up very foolishly in many ways, and so I've always said. Through it you've become a shocking little madam, but you'll suffer for it. Pride comes before a fall, you'll see."

Lalla swallowed a lump in her throat. If only Nana would understand it was not that she was being a madam! But Nana could not, it was no good trying to explain. She turned away to the window, blinking to keep back tears which wanted to run down her cheeks. It made things more awful than ever if Nana was turning against her.

It was not only Nana who seemed to Lalla to be turning against her, it was everybody, and the worst turner-against was Harriet. Harriet had done her best. It was not easy being friendly with Lalla when she was in a state. If she talked about skating Lalla would say something like "What do you know about it anyway?" and if she did not talk about skating Lalla got suspicious. "Why do you try and not talk about my test? I suppose Max has told you not to. You two are always talking to each other, jabber, jabber, jabber. I guessed you were talking about me."

In the few weeks Lalla thought her medicine was working it had been all right. Harriet had her usual fun with Lalla. They talked all the time when they were not at lessons, and rushed out every day to look at Alec's strawberries. But when the effect of the medicine wore off Harriet found the only thing to do was to keep out of Lalla's way as much as possible, and talk to her as little as possible. She did not want to have a row with her, and she knew she would in the end. Nobody could go on giving soft answers that were supposed to turn away wrath, when the wrath went on coming at you just the same.

As it happened, Harriet did not feel talkish as her inter-silver test day came nearer. During the last six months the little-girl Harriet, without her noticing it, had disappeared and a new Harriet had taken her place. A Harriet who looked much the same outside, but was more of a person inside.

Everybody noticed it. Miss Goldthorpe told Nana it was a

pleasure having Harriet about, she was becoming interesting to
talk to. Nana said she didn't know about talking, but it was more
worth while to dress Harriet, she looked really nice now at the
rink in the new things Nana had knitted for her. Alonso Vittori,
watching Harriet, murmured, "It's a funny little personality but
she's got something, that child." Monsieur Cordon said of Harriet
to Miss Goldthorpe, "*Un type curieux!*" At the rink she stopped being just the little girl Mr. Matthews allowed to skate free, or the
child Lalla Moore's aunt had taken up, and became Harriet Johnson, one of Max Lindblom's promising pupils.

As the day of the test came nearer, Harriet was more and
more wrapped up in skating, and noticed less and less what people were thinking or saying. She had private plans. If she passed
the inter-silver—and she knew it was a big "if"—she would tell
the family. How surprised they would be! But telling them would
be just the beginning of her idea.

If she passed—she held her thumbs when she thought of
it—perhaps this autumn she could try for the silver, and if she
passed that, the next spring attempt the inter-gold, and have a try
for the gold six months later. That would mean, if she got on as
fast as that, she would have her first try for the gold the autumn
she was thirteen; and allowing for lots of failures, she might have
passed everything by the time she was fifteen. Even if she didn't
pass them all she would have a lovely career when she was old
enough. She would be a professional skater, like that girl skating
on one foot in the poster she had seen just before it was first
planned she should go to the rink. Nobody must know what she
was planning or they would laugh at her (which was natural,
while she was no better than she was now), but she was sure if she
worked she would get better. Then she would surprise the boys
by earning money much sooner than they could.

Harriet's was a very full day. Every morning she caught the bus in time to reach Lalla's house by a quarter to nine. The moment Wilson let her in she rushed up to Nana to change and was in the schoolroom by nine. After lessons there was ballet, fencing, a walk sometimes, gardening or shopping for Lalla. Then lunch. Then the rink, Max's lessons, and hard practice. Then home and homework, for now that she and Lalla were eleven and a half, more lessons had to be squeezed in, so having tea with each other had to come to an end. After lessons came supper and bed. When there was thinking and planning a future as well, there was not much room for other people's troubles, and that was how the quarrel with Lalla started.

Rinks draw press photographers. Lalla was so used to being photographed that she broke off whatever she was doing, posed charmingly, and skated off as casually as if she had only stopped to sneeze. But one day a photographer noticed Harriet.

"Who's the little ginger-haired girl?"

Somebody explained. "A pupil of Max Lindblom's. Only been skating about eighteen months. He thinks a lot of her."

The photographer took an action photograph of Harriet practicing a back change. It was a lucky photograph, for Harriet looked charmingly serious. The photographer's paper published it over the caption "Little Harriet Johnson, for whom a great future is predicted." It was an evening paper, and of course somebody saw the photograph. Harriet was having a lesson at the time, so the picture was shown to Lalla. Lalla said how nice it was, and she must buy a copy for Harriet, but inside she was furious. Harriet! Poor little Harriet who wore Lalla's clothes, and had her lessons paid for to keep Lalla company, sneaking around and getting her photograph taken! The bit about her future was idiotic, of course, for Harriet had no future. It was the meanness of it she minded.

Now that she came to think of it, Harriet was being mean all round. As the angry thoughts flew round in Lalla's head, she skated faster and faster as if she were in a relay race. "Mean! Mean! Mean!" But if Harriet was going to treat her like that, she would show her.

When Harriet, knowing nothing about the photograph, skated back on to the private rink, Lalla, her face scarlet, dragged her into a corner.

"Look at that!"

Harriet stared at the photograph. Her! Her in a paper! Then she saw what the paper had written.

"Oh, bother! I never knew it was being taken, or I wouldn't have let them."

"Why not?"

"Because the family might see it, and I don't want to tell them I'm taking tests or anything. I want to surprise them."

Lalla looked at Harriet, and a stab shot through her. Surprise them! Suppose she did! Suppose she could! Suppose . . . but she would not think of that. She was frightened at her half thought, and so worried and miserable she could have cried. But she was too proud to do that in public, and anyway she knew of something better to make Harriet feel as awful as she herself was feeling.

"You'd better keep this photograph, for it's most likely the only one they'll ever take of you. If you pass your inter-silver, I'll tell Aunt Claudia I don't want you to work with me any more."

CHAPTER 14

The Thermometer Rises

HARRIET FELT AS an insect must feel who flies round and round a room unable to find a way out. What was she to do? If she told Max she would not enter for her inter-silver he would just flick his fingers, and tell her not to be silly. She could not explain to Miss Goldthorpe or Nana; they would be furious with Lalla, who would think her a mean beast to tell tales, which she would be. In any case it would do no good; neither Nana, Goldie nor anyone else could make Aunt Claudia let her go on sharing things with Lalla if Lalla said she didn't want her.

Nor could she tell her family. First of all they wouldn't understand; they had never heard she was going in for her inter-silver, so all they would say would be "Well, don't enter for the inter-silver if Lalla's cross about it," not seeing that if you learned from Max Lindblom you couldn't just say "I'm not entering," without making him understand why. Also she couldn't tell her family because of Lalla. They thought Lalla was sometimes a bit grand; but they all liked her and talked about her as if she were part of the family. It would be horrible to have to tell them what Lalla had threatened and why. It would make the boys turn against her; they probably wouldn't even pick the strawberries they had grown in her garden. Olivia, who not only liked but really loved Lalla, would find it hard to forgive her.

The terrible thing was that Harriet had to make up her mind quickly. Having made her threat, Lalla wouldn't speak any more. She and Harriet had practiced at different ends of the private rink until it was time to go home. Outside the rink Nana said good-bye to Harriet and Harriet said good-bye to Nana; it had not been noticeable, Harriet thought, that Lalla did not say "See you tomorrow" or "Bet I get my homework finished sooner than you do," or something usual of that sort.

To make up her mind what to do Harriet walked home by the longest way she knew, and just before she reached home she found the answer. She couldn't tell Max she would not try for her inter-silver after he had worked so hard to make it possible, and she couldn't let Lalla tell Aunt Claudia she didn't want her to learn things from her. It would not be true; Lalla would be miserable doing things all alone again, but being Lalla, having threatened to say something, she would say it, even if it hurt her. Harriet got a lump in her throat when she thought of not learning things with Lalla. No more Nana! No more Goldie! Never to see Lalla again! It couldn't be. No more dancing! No more fencing! It was at that thought, although it was not a cold evening, that Harriet shivered. *No more skating!* She could go to the rink and practice, but she knew she never would. How could she practice at the rink where Lalla was? It was not to be thought of. Lalla must be given in to, and no one but Lalla must know why she was unable to take the test.

When Harriet reached home only Olivia was in. She was in the kitchen.

"Hullo, darling. You're first. Edward's gone to tea with one of his admiring old ladies. Toby's in the shop with Daddy, and Alec, of course, is doing his papers."

Harriet leaned against the kitchen door. "I'm going up to bed."

Olivia was cutting a loaf. She put down the knife and came over to Harriet. "Are you ill, pet?"

Harriet hated lying to Olivia. "I feel sort of funny-ish."

"Where?"

"Just all-overish."

Olivia took Harriet's satchel of books from her.

"Let me help you up to your room, darling. I dare say it's nothing. I expect you're overtired; I was only saying to Daddy last night what a busy life you led, and how I hoped it wouldn't be too much for you."

Lying in bed, trying to look ill, and feeling mean at being waited on when she was perfectly well, Harriet heard the rest of the family return one by one.

First Toby and George, talking cheerfully as they came upstairs, then silent, then whispering. Olivia would be telling them about her, and warning them to keep quiet in case she was asleep. Presently Edward came home.

"Mummy! Mummy! I've had a gorgeous tea, and Mrs. Pinker said she wished she could adopt me."

Toby came out, his whisper as carrying as Edward's shout. "Shut up. Harriet's ill. I should think Dad and Mum would be glad if Mrs. Pinker would take a conceited little rat like you."

It was when Alec came home that everybody forgot to be quiet. He raced up the stairs shouting. "Mum! Dad! Everybody! Look at this. Where's Harriet?"

They all talked at once. "Let me look, Toby, I'm shorter than you, so you can see over me."

"All right, Edward, but don't shove or you'll tear it."

Olivia read out loud: "'Little Harriet Johnson, for whom a great future is predicted.'"

George was amazed. "That's never my Harriet?"

Then Olivia: "She's not well, poor pet, but I think this will cheer her up. I'll see if she's awake."

The photograph! Because of the quarrel with Lalla Harriet had quite forgotten the photograph. But of course Alec would see it. It was on the front page of the paper, and he would notice it as he folded the papers to put them in the letter-boxes.

It was dreadfully difficult to pretend to be ill when all the family sat round the bed looking proud and admiring.

"But what's all this, darling, about the future?" Olivia asked. "I didn't know you could skate properly yet."

"I can't, it's just something to say."

Alec re-read the caption. "Somebody must have said you had a great future."

Toby's brain was working. "How many girls go to your rink, Harriet?"

"I don't know, dozens and dozens."

"Well, if five dozen girls skate at a rink, and a photographer photographs the eight most promising."

"Don't bother the child with mathematics," said Olivia. "It's obvious, though she won't say so, that somebody does think she's promising."

Alec sat down on the bed. "What about those tests Lalla does? Will you have to do those?"

Harriet felt a huge lump form in her throat. What fun this evening would have been if she could have said she was taking her inter-silver at the beginning of next month.

"I took my preliminary and bronze before Christmas."

There was a family howl. "Slyboots," said Alec.

Edward looked reproving. "If it was me who was passing tests, I'd tell everybody."

"I bet you would," said Toby, "but Harriet's not a bragger like you, thank goodness."

"What comes next?" asked George. "I mean, there's a silver-something Lalla passed, isn't there?"

"Yes, pet," said Olivia, "what comes next? Tell us everything. We're so full of pride and curiosity."

Everything! Oh, if she only could! Harriet tried to say inter-silver, and that perhaps she would try for it in the autumn. But would she? Would Lalla ever let her try for it? She struggled hard against the wave of misery that flowed over her, but it was no use. Her eyes filled with tears, she rolled over on her pillows and cried dreadfully.

Olivia, finding that Harriet had no temperature, decided she was just tired and that a day or two in bed would put her right, so she rang up Lalla's house and asked Wilson, who answered the telephone, to let Nana and Miss Goldthorpe know. But when it came to the fourth day, and Harriet just lay in bed and wouldn't attempt to get up, Olivia became worried.

"It's so unlike her," she said to George, "I'm going to get Doctor Phillipson to have a look at her."

Harriet had been afraid of that. She made a plan. As soon as Olivia went down to see what Uncle William had sent for the shop, Harriet nipped down to the kitchen, boiled a kettle, and filled a hot-water bottle. When Doctor Phillipson arrived he did what he usually did, put his thermometer in Harriet's mouth, and while it was there, talked to Olivia. That was Harriet's chance. She took the thermometer out of her mouth, and laid it on the hot-water bottle.

Doctor Phillipson seemed to be able to time taking temperatures without looking at a watch. Harriet trembled as she saw he was going to take the thermometer out of her mouth. Would it have gone up enough degrees for him to say she was ill?

Doctor Phillipson looked at the thermometer for longer than usual. Then he looked at Harriet. Then he gave the thermometer a shake. Then he rummaged in his case and handed some instruments to Olivia.

"I shall examine her. Would you boil these for ten minutes?"

When the door had shut behind Olivia, Doctor Phillipson sat down on the bed. He spoke in a friendly whisper. "What's up?" Harriet tried to look as if she did not know what he meant, but she failed dismally. He took one of her hands. "I thought we were friends. You may as well confide in me, because if you want to stay in bed you'll need co-operation."

"How did you know I wasn't ill?"

"I thought you were all right when I looked at you, but when I found your temperature was so high the quicksilver had run up out of sight, I knew you must be malingering, for if the thermometer was speaking the truth you'd be dead."

Harriet saw she was caught. It was no good trying to deceive Doctor Phillipson, and it was true he was a friend.

"If I tell you what's happened you must swear not to tell anybody. It's something really terrible."

The relief of telling everything made Harriet feel happier than she had since the quarrel. When she had finished Doctor Phillipson got up and walked over to the window, thinking hard. After a bit he made up his mind.

"I think it might be possible to sort things out for Lalla as well as for yourself; and she needs help badly, poor child."

Harriet was surprised that Doctor Phillipson was nice about

Lalla; she had expected him to say she had behaved like a little beast.

"It wouldn't mean her telling Aunt Claudia I'm not to learn with her any more?"

"No. But it will mean several people will have to know what's happened."

Harriet did not like that. "Will I have to tell them? Lalla will think me an awful sneak."

The Doctor rumpled her hair. "Lalla will do most of the telling. Now take that worried look off your face and trust me."

Lalla had been as bothered as Harriet had been about meeting after the quarrel. She did not want Goldie or Nana knowing there had been a quarrel. "Not that I mind what they think," she told herself, "they're sure to side with Harriet. Everybody sides with Harriet just because she's so mimsy-pimsy and good." But telling herself that sort of thing didn't help. A voice in her head, which she could not talk down, told her that she would mind dreadfully if Nana and Goldie knew what she had said to Harriet, because they would both be ashamed of her. It was a relief when Wilson came up the next morning with Olivia's message. It was sensible of Harriet to pretend she was ill. Lalla even had to admit to herself it was clever. If Harriet said she was ill she wouldn't be allowed to go in for her inter-silver test, and when it was certain she was not going in, Lalla would be nice to her again.

In spite of the voice in her head which nagged at her, telling her how badly she had behaved, Lalla got through the next three days pretty well, she thought. She answered inquiries about Harriet in an ordinary voice, and was sure nobody suspected it was anything to do with her that was making Harriet stay in bed. Then on the fourth day she had a shock. Each morning Miss

Goldthorpe rang up and asked how Harriet was, and each morning Olivia said in a casual way there was nothing much the matter, but on the fourth morning Olivia sounded worried.

"She seems all right, but I can't get her out of bed, so I'm getting Doctor Phillipson to look at her."

When Lalla heard this a cold feeling like drips of icy water ran down her back. Doctor Phillipson! His medicine had not done much good, but she knew he was clever. He wouldn't be fooled into thinking a person was ill when she was not, and he wouldn't say Harriet was not to take a test, unless he thought she was ill. What was Harriet going to do now? She couldn't be such a mean dog as to tell the truth!

All morning the thought of Harriet's seeing the doctor made Lalla feel wobbly inside and made her hands damp. Not that she was ashamed of what she had said—of course she wasn't—but she wouldn't want everybody knowing. They didn't understand about skating, and so wouldn't see how sly Harriet had been. At the end of lessons she said in as uninterested a voice as she could manage:

"While I'm putting on my coat would you telephone Mrs. Johnson, Goldie dear, and ask what the doctor said?"

When Lalla came back to the schoolroom dressed to go out, Miss Goldthorpe seemed sad and grave.

"I'm afraid it's bad news, dear. Harriet's dreadfully ill. The doctor told Mrs. Johnson he had never known any body to live whose temperature showed so high a reading."

Lalla gaped at Miss Goldthorpe. Harriet very ill! Harriet with so high a temperature she might be going to die!

It couldn't be true. Harriet had been perfectly well five days ago. She wasn't ill now, only pretending because she wanted a reason not to take her inter-silver.

"What's the matter with her?"

"The doctor can't say. Mrs. Johnson asked if she had been working too hard. She says she's worrying about something. She's talked a lot about you, and an inter-silver test."

Lalla licked her lips which had gone very dry. "What did she say about me?"

"Mrs. Johnson didn't say. Rambling, I expect, poor child."

Lalla felt most peculiar. Worrying! Inter-silver! What had she done? She heard bells ringing somewhere and suddenly Goldie was behaving in a very odd way, far off one minute, and near the next. Then everything spun round, and she felt herself falling.

Lalla opened her eyes to find herself lying on her bed; Nana was dabbing *eau de Cologne* on her forehead.

"There, there! This won't do. It won't help Harriet if you get ill."

Slowly everything came back to Lalla. Tears oozed in a tired way out of her eyes. "She's terribly ill, Nana. She's got so high a temperature she might die."

"Nonsense, dear, you weren't meant to take it so serious. For all she's so frail-looking, Harriet's tough. You look more like dying; green as a lettuce you are."

Miss Goldthorpe came hurrying in carrying a glass. "Here's the brandy. I've rung for the doctor; he'll be along in a minute."

Lalla, though she still felt very come-and-go-ish, sat up.

"I won't see the doctor. He'll say I've to stay in today, and I won't. I must see Harriet."

Miss Goldthorpe put an arm round her and held the brandy to her lips. "Sip this. You couldn't see Harriet anyway. Her doctor said you weren't to see her unless he gave you permission."

Lalla choked over the brandy. "I must. This is disgusting stuff."

Nana took the glass from Miss Goldthorpe. "Nonsense, dear. You drink it up. I don't hold with spirits as a rule, but for fainting, brandy's good."

Lalla knew it was no good arguing with Nana about medicine. If she said "swallow" then swallow it was. She finished the brandy and at once felt better.

"If I see the doctor, will you ring Harriet's doctor, Goldie, and say I must, absolutely must, see Harriet?"

"Very well, dear, but it can't be today. I'm sure you've got to stay in bed today."

"Of course you have," Nana agreed. "Fainting indeed! That's something quite uncalled for and not what I like from a child of mine."

Lalla's doctor was old and rather grumpy, but he was a good doctor. When he saw Lalla he was not at all pleased; he told Nana to undress her and he would examine her thoroughly. The examining took a long time; it seemed to Lalla that there was no bit of her he was not interested in. At last she got cross.

"I've nothing the matter with my eyes, so there's no need to pull them about; and my knees are quite well, so there's no need hitting them to see if my legs bounce."

But Lalla might just as well have kept quiet. The doctor did not care what she said but went on calmly with his examination. At the end he packed his case.

"She's to stay there, Nurse, until I give her leave to get up. Now, where's Mrs. King? I want to see her."

Lalla spoke pleadingly. "Don't be all doctor-ish. What are you going to tell Aunt Claudia?"

The doctor came back to the bed. He pointed at the skating shoes in the glass case, and to the text.

"There's to be no more of that business for quite a time.

You're thoroughly run down, young woman. I'm telling your aunt
you're to go away somewhere bracing."

"I can't just now, my friend Harriet's ill, and I've got a skating test."

The doctor made a tush noise. "There will be no more skating tests for many months. I can promise you that."

Nana went out of the room with the doctor. Lalla lay as still
in bed as if she had been carved in wood, waiting to feel the effect
of the frightful words the doctor had just uttered. When that happened she would do something—dash downstairs, make a scene,
tell Aunt Claudia not to listen, that she was going to take her test
no matter what anybody said. But although she lay as still as still
for a long time, and understood in every inch of her what the doctor had ordered, she didn't get angry, or dash anywhere. Instead
she felt as if she had been carrying a weight on her back which
was far too heavy for her, and somebody had quietly lifted it off
and said "Don't bother with that. Sit down and rest."

She had not given in to anybody about the test. The doctor
didn't even know about her trouble with loops. She had fainted.
She was run down. She wasn't to skate, she was to go away for a
holiday. In the autumn, after the holiday, she would take the test.
There would be nobody whispering "Lalla isn't taking her test because she isn't ready for it." Nobody saying "Lalla Moore's not doing as well as everybody expected, is she?" Nobody could say
anything but the truth: "Lalla isn't taking her test because she's terribly run down. She fainted, absolutely unconscious." As in imagination she heard the dramatic story of her faint passed round the
rink, Lalla almost said "Giggerty-geggerty," but before the "gig"
was in her head she remembered Harriet. Harriet with the highest
temperature anybody ever had all because of what she had said to
her! Poor, poor Harriet! And they wouldn't let her see her,

wouldn't let her say she was sorry and that of course Harriet could take the inter-silver test if only she'd get well.

Miss Goldthorpe came in. She drew a chair up to the bed. She sat down looking cozy and like somebody who was in no hurry. "This is upsetting. No skating for a bit."

Lalla brushed the skating aside. "Goldie, I've got to see Harriet, absolutely got to."

"Why, dear?"

Lalla wriggled. "I can't explain why but I've got to."

"I can't help you then. I thought perhaps you could send a message by me to Mrs. Johnson. She could have passed on whatever it is you want to say to Harriet, but if it's a secret it will have to wait until both you and Harriet are better."

Lalla bounced in the bed with impatience. "I'm not ill. I fainted, which I never did before, but that's not having the highest temperature anyone ever had without being dead."

Miss Goldthorpe looked fondly at Lalla. "Don't you think you could trust me and Harriet's mother with the message? It can't be as secret as all that, can it?"

Lalla saw she would have to admit at least part of the truth. "It's something I said that's made her ill."

"You! What did you say?"

Lalla was still feeling peculiar after her faint, and deadly worried. Her voice rose in a howl. "Oh, Goldie, I've been an awful beast, the nastiest beast that ever, ever was. You'll despise me forever and ever. . . ."

Miss Goldthorpe sat on the bed, her arms round Lalla, and heard the shocking story. It was difficult to hear it through Lalla's chokes and sobs. At the end she lent Lalla her handkerchief, and brushed her hair off her face.

"You'd better tell Mrs. Johnson all this, and she can tell Harriet how sorry you are. And I'm afraid you'll have to tell Nana. You see, the doctor said you were to be kept quiet and Nana won't let Mrs. Johnson in unless she knows how important it is."

Lalla gave her nose an enormous blow.

"All right. I'll tell Nana too. I'll tell everybody anybody likes. I'll even tell Harriet's brothers if she wants me to, and that would be awful, especially Toby, who's always been a bit despising."

Nana sat by Lalla's bed knitting and heard the confession. Occasionally she shook her head or made a clicking noise with her tongue against her teeth. At the end she said:

"It was wrong of you, dear, and you know it, but if Harriet's well in time she can take that test, and no harm done."

"But she couldn't be well in time, not with the highest temperature in the world."

Nana went back to her knitting. "I shouldn't wonder. Funny things, temperatures. Now you stop fretting and it'll be all right. You'll see."

Olivia had been shocked to hear of Lalla's faint, and came round as quickly as possible. Although she had to keep her promise to Doctor Phillipson and not tell Lalla that Harriet wasn't ill at all, she couldn't let her go on worrying.

"Harriet's better, pet."

"Oh good! Will you tell her I'm awfully sorry? I didn't mean what I said—at least I did then, but I don't any more—and please tell her she can do her inter-silver test if she's well in time. Do you think she will be?"

I shouldn't wonder. Olivia took off her coat and gloves and sat down. "Suppose you tell me all about it." Not by a flick of an eyelash did Olivia let Lalla know she already knew the story. She

wanted to hear it again, for only in that way could she help Lalla.
At the end she asked: "Why did you mind about the photograph?
You've had so many taken.

Lalla pleated her eiderdown while she tried to explain.

"It wasn't the photographs . . . , it was those loops I told you
about. . . . I hoped I couldn't do them because I'd outgrown my
strength, like you said, but it wasn't that. . . ."

"What was it?"

Lalla struggled with herself. It was what she had never ad-
mitted, and had never meant to admit. "I just couldn't do them.
They were too difficult."

Olivia jumped up and kissed her. "Bless you, my pet, I've
been longing to hear you say that."

Lalla wriggled away. "Why?"

"Don't be cross. I don't know anything about skating; you
may be the great skater of the future, I don't know, but ever since
that matinée we went to together I do know you've been worrying
too much about it. Miss Goldthorpe tells me you're not to skate
for awhile, and I think it very good news. You might find it isn't
the only thing you want to do."

Lalla threw her chin into the air. "I won't. You see, I've got
to be something important and how else would I be except by
skating?"

Olivia put on her coat. "I must get back to Harriet. I don't
know, but I have an idea that if, for a little, you would stop thinking about being a skating champion, you might find out that it
wasn't so important as you thought."

# CHAPTER 15

The Future

AUNT CLAUDIA RENTED a cottage on a lonely part of the southeast coast, and moved Lalla, Harriet, Miss Goldthorpe and Nana into it. The doctor said there were to be very few lessons for Lalla, so sitting-round-the-table lessons only happened on wet days. On fine days she and Harriet went about doing just what they liked, wearing scarcely any clothes, and getting browner and browner every day. Every night Lalla went to sleep the moment her head touched the pillow, and she did not wake until Nana came in and drew back her curtains. She ate the most enormous amount of food, including all the things Aunt Claudia had said made a person fat, and although she got fatter nobody cared.

"Anyway," Lalla said, "I don't go on getting fatter. I just got fatter to start with and now I've stuck to that size."

Harriet too had an enormous appetite, but she remained thin, and nobody minded that either.

"You're that kind, dear," Nana said. "You won't fatten, not if you ate forty meals a day."

To begin with Harriet was told not to talk about skating to Lalla, but that soon wore off, for Lalla would talk about it. She had not been at the rink to watch Harriet when she had passed her inter-silver test, but she loved teasing her and showing her how she must have looked taking it. She would pull down the corners of her mouth.

"Watch me, Harriet. This is you waiting to begin. Now this is you doing your back change. Here's you doing your threes. This is your one-foot eight. And this is you trying not to show how much you want to look at your tracings."

Lalla was funny enough imitating skating on ice, but with bare feet on wet sand she was so silly that Harriet would laugh so much that it hurt. Then Lalla would laugh too, and they would have to lie down or they would have fallen over.

But as she got better and gayer, Lalla began to think. Not the frightened, dashing-from-side-to-side kind of thinking, but sensible thinking; and what she thought came out in things she said to Harriet.

"I shan't try for my inter-gold until Max says I'm ready. . . . Down here without Aunt Claudia I can see it's silly to rush and get in a state. . . . I don't think even by working hard from September on I'll get those loathsome change loops right this year. I don't care a bit if I wait till May . . ." Then suddenly one morning she said: "Harriet, d'you know what I'm going to do? I'm going to write to Uncle David at his office, so Aunt Claudia won't know I've written, and get him to see Max and ask him when he thinks I'll be ready to take the inter-gold. I'd rather know than not know. If Max says not till May, Uncle David can tell Aunt Claudia for me while they're in Canada in August. Canada's a gloriously long way off. I wouldn't know what she was saying and I wouldn't care."

There was no answer for some time to Lalla's letter except a postcard saying "O.K., poppet." Then suddenly Uncle David telephoned. Lalla answered the phone; they could tell by her excited squeaks something nice was going to happen.

"All of them! What fun! Lucky them, I wish we could. In the car! Giggerty-geggerty, I must tell Harriet, I can't wait."

It was wonderful news. Uncle David had taken rooms near the cottage for Olivia and George for a week, and for himself for a night. For the boys a tent was coming and they were to camp in it all of August. Uncle David was bringing the Johnsons by car.

A week later they all arrived. At first there was such a lot to say that it seemed they would never catch up with one another's news. Over the tent putting-up, at which Lalla and Harriet helped, Alec told of the wonderful thing that had happened to him. Mr. Pulton had seen George and said he would like to send Alec to an agricultural college, and that when Alec had finished training he, Mr. Pulton, would invest some money in a market garden. He had said that he would like to help make somebody else's dream come true, because it was too late now to find his own.

"And I'll tell you one reason why he said that," said Toby. "It's because Alec took him some of our strawberries. My word, Lalla, they've been stupendous. Simpson's been marvelous. He's picked them for us every day and had them ready when Edward and I went to fetch them."

Harriet was terribly pleased about Alec. "That'll mean more chance for you, Toby. You can go somewhere like Oxford and be a professor of mathematics, for Alec won't cost anything."

Edward was knocking in a tent peg. At this he stopped and looked in a pained way at Harriet. "There is me. I shan't go to a university because by then I'll be a film star . . ."

The rest of what Edward had to say was lost. They all fell on him and rolled him in the sand.

That night it was fine. They had supper on the beach. While it was being cooked Lalla and Uncle David went for a walk. Lalla, in spite of trying not to care, felt wormish inside.

"What did Max say?" she asked.

Uncle David lit a cigarette. "There's to be no thought of your going in for that test you were working for until next year."

Lalla was frightened to ask the next question, but she made herself do it. "Did he say anything else?"

Uncle David took her hand. "Prepare yourself for a shock, poppet. He doesn't see you as a world champion. He says you'll never be a good enough figure skater."

Lalla stopped. Her eyes were frightened. "But I couldn't just be ordinary, I'm not used to it."

Uncle David laughed. "You won't be. We've got ideas, that Max of yours and I. Anyway there's nothing for you to worry about. You go back to your skating as usual in the autumn."

Lalla could sense that Uncle David was happy about her. "Tell me what you and Max have thought of. I can feel it's something nice."

"There's something else first which you've got to know. It's about Harriet. Max thinks she's a find."

Lalla gasped. "Harriet! Do you mean it might be she who's a 'champion grim' and not me?"

"Might. It's too early yet to say. But don't think that means you're out of the picture. You're not. You'll like Max Lindblom's idea for you."

Lalla was impatient. "Well, why don't you tell me what it is?"

"I've got your Aunt Claudia to talk round. You know, it's been tough on her not being allowed to discuss skating with you."

"But I ought to know; it's my future."

"Don't take that tone with me, young woman, or I'll drop you in the sea. Now listen. How would you like to be a professional skater?"

When Lalla and Uncle David got back to the picnic, supper

was almost cooked. Olivia and Nana were tasting some soup they were boiling over a fire of driftwood.

"There you are, Lalla," George called out. "Harriet says you'll give us an imitation of her on the ice."

Lalla was delighted; she felt so gay, just in the mood to make people laugh. An audience again! It made her tingle as if it were Christmas Eve. She ran on to the sand and not only imitated Harriet, but Max, a fat judge trying to keep warm, and Mr. Matthews nearly falling over as he presented a bouquet. She had a perfect audience; everybody laughed until they could not laugh any more.

"You must stop, Lalla darling," said Olivia, drying her eyes, "or I shall upset the soup."

Lalla knelt by Olivia and looked at the soup. "I wish that was a witches' brew, and you could see things that are going to happen. Uncle David says he's told you Harriet's more likely to be a 'champion grim' than I am."

Edward peered into the soup. "See that bubble? That's you, Lalla, getting awfully important?'

Uncle David had a look at the bubble. "I shouldn't wonder. I can see Lalla as a professional. She's got what it takes, and she can be funny too. The world is short of funny queens of the ice."

Edward gave a squeak. "Look at that piece of carrot that's come to the top! That's Harriet skating with one leg stuck out behind her."

Olivia gave the piece of carrot a little push. "My Harriet skating to the stars? I can't see that happening."

Lalla looked in the soup. "I can. I expect Aunt Claudia will help."

Harriet could hardly believe all she had heard. Max thought she might make a star skater! Lalla not minding! She tried to put her thoughts into words:

"I feel curiouser and curiouser—nearly twelve, which is old enough to start proper training, and perhaps for something gorgeous to happen."

Lalla felt mad-doggish with gayness. A professional! She would have to be able to do all the figures of course, but after that, free skating forever and ever, and an audience to watch her do it.

"Giggerty-geggerty, I can't wait. Imagine if that soup could show the future. Don't you all want to know what happens to Harriet and me? Because I do."